The Burning Fire of Greed

A tale of murder and revenge

BOOK ONE

AGNES MAKÓCZY

For information contact :
www.agnes-makoczy.com

Book Cover Image by Šárka Jonášová from Pixabay
fjord77
https://pixabay.com/photos/girl-flower-spring-april-flowers-5019894/

Book formatting by Derek Murphy from www.CreativIndie.com

ISBN: 0-9774395-7-7
First Edition: August 2016

Contents

Chapter 1 18

Chapter 2 23

Chapter 3 28

Chapter 4 30

Chapter 5 35

Chapter 6 40

Chapter 7 43

Chapter 8 46

Chapter 9 49

Chapter 10 58

Chapter 11 61

Chapter 12 64

Chapter 13 67

Chapter 14 78

Chapter 15 83

Chapter 16 90

Chapter 17 94

Chapter 18 101

Chapter 19 102

Chapter 20 113

Chapter 21 118

Chapter 22 121

Chapter 23 124

Chapter 24 127

Chapter 25 131

Chapter 26 145

Chapter 27 154

Chapter 28 157

Chapter 29 160

Chapter 30 166

Chapter 31 169

Chapter 32 171

Chapter 33 175

Chapter 34 178

Chapter 35 182

Chapter 36 184

Chapter 37 189

Chapter 38 195

Chapter 39 197

Chapter 40 201

Chapter 41 204

Chapter 42 207

The Vanishing Bloodstain 208

About the Author 211

INTRODUCTION

HE LEANED AGAINST THE TRUNK of the old oak tree and positioned himself behind the azaleas to remain in semi-shadows. He was getting impatient, tired of waiting, but he was too scared to disappoint her. He was terrified of how easily she changed. One minute she was sweet, making him promises, getting so close to him that he could smell her expensive perfume and go insane with desire. The next minute, she would get increasingly agitated, even if it was a minor infraction, and as big and strong as he was, he would cringe and cower, not knowing really how to handle her. In those moments, she would fling a glass or an ashtray in his direction, anything she could get her hands on, and scream, and threaten him, and call him names. But as soon as she calmed down, he would be her sweetheart again. No, he mustn't make her angry. If he had to stay behind the azaleas all night, so be it.

The sun was hanging low on the horizon now, and the bugs came out in droves. He felt things crawling on his neck, his arms, up the legs of his trousers, and he quelled the desire to run. The mosquitos—especially—loved his black clothes and his spicy aftershave, and wouldn't leave him alone. He swept them away from his face, he slapped them dead on his arms, but more kept coming, buzzing, excited, puncturing his skin with savage glee, getting in his ears, his nose, even in his eyes. It was worse than torment.

He was almost on the verge of giving up when a sudden movement startled him and made him look. Someone had opened the front door to the hotel, and the sounds of classical music and laughter came pouring out into the dark spot where he stood. It must be her, so young, so innocent. A stranger. He had never seen her before except in a grainy photograph. He wasn't sure it was her. He wasn't even sure that he would be capable of hurting her, but what choice did he have? It was too late to back out. *And make it look like an accident*, he'd been told, which made it even harder, because he was strong enough to snap someone's neck with his bare hands if he had to, but planning a murder that looked like an accident, well, you needed cunning and forethought for that, and he just wasn't good at such things.

He watched the girl as she walked to the park. Mesmerized by her youth and her naivety, his hands clenched and unclenched—as if in practice—itching to squeeze something, and he imagined how it would feel to snap her slender neck in his bare hands.

He pushed the idea away, violently. He was not that kind of a person. No. He was gentle, and he was kind. He would be incapable. And yet, he couldn't take his eyes off of her as she sat on the bench by the water and ate something she had in her hands, chatting with some guy sitting next to her. He could feel the good and the evil inside him, fighting for his soul, and wished he had the courage to walk away.

But on he stayed. He watched her get up and walk along the beach and head for the lookout. That excited him. It opened a new possibility. It gave him hope. Maybe up there he would get his chance. There had been numerous accidents where the edge of the salt cliffs had crumbled into the sea. Innocent tourists had fallen onto the sharp rocks below and had been smashed to bits. Nobody would suspect foul play, not with a kid from out of town.

He steeled himself for murder and stepped out softly from behind the bushes. It was important to be careful and not be seen. He looked around quickly and saw that they were all alone. Moving like a shadow in the penumbra, he followed her, grinning with excitement. This wouldn't be too bad at all.

RECITAL

NICOLA FONTAINE, MAGNIFICENT in her blood-red velvet concert dress and the famous Maharani of Krishnaraja jewels that she always wore for performances, stepped up to the podium and took her place next to the shiny black piano. She allowed the silent room to admire her for a few seconds—standing as still as a marble statue, an arm elegantly resting on the edge of the piano—and then she smiled. The Prodigal Daughter was back in Half Moon Bay after a twenty-year absence in which she, the Sublime Fontaine, had become a world-renowned opera singer, fêted by the rich and the royals alike. Next to her—small and almost insignificant—stood Ava Sigur, the Alto to her Soprano, in a white satin evening gown that didn't do much to complement her fair complexion.

Nicola batted her eyelashes at the musicians of the chamber orchestra behind her, touched the fabulous necklace at her throat for good luck, and then nodded to them. The room fell silent, the crackling of programs ceased, and the people settled down. Slowly, the myriad lights in the chandeliers overhead dimmed, and then they went dark.

The moment Nicola began singing Lakmé's *Sous le dôme épais*, Léo Delibes' famous Flower Duet, the audience—surprised at the warmth of her voice and the beauty of the music—stopped fidgeting and whispering, and allowed themselves to be carried away by the story of Lakmé and her servant Mallika as they gather flowers by the river. The musicians, just as infatuated by Nicola's beauty and artistry as the audience, smiled to themselves as they dreamed of Oriental lands and mysterious adventures hinted at by the enthralling, exotic music, and Nicola's bewitching voice.

Ava Sigur, the Alto—so pale and small standing next to her—did her best to appear confident and keep up with the other woman, joining Nicola in a pristine and impeccable duet. Yet her eyes kept darting sideways, betraying the intimidation she felt at having to perform next to this formidable woman. And Margo Fontaine—her daughter—who knew what it felt like to be dwarfed by the talents of the Sublime Fontaine, felt sorry for her. She knew better than anyone that you could just never quite measure up to someone like her mother.

Once the recital was over, the mesmerized crowd stood up as one, pushing chairs to the floor, letting programs float away, to give the Sublime Fontaine a standing ovation shouting *Brava, Brava* and rushed to the podium, pushing each other out of the way, and stepping on shoes and hanging shawls to congratulate her mother.

Margo smiled, thinking about how awesome her mom was, feeling so proud of her. This was a ritual she knew well, having been through it hundreds, maybe thousands of times, but it never got old, seeing her mom so excited and so happy. Nicola would receive flowers and praise, and breathe in gratefully the admiration of the audience. This was—after all—what she lived for. One more time Margo would be forgotten while her mom, surrounded by her admirers, autographed programs and smiled graciously as she received their compliments. And at the back of the room, Margo would wait patiently for someone to remember that she too existed.

But boy, it was hot in there. Her shirt was getting wetter and heavier by the minute. She fanned herself with the program and wished she could be somewhere else. People kept pushing her to the side, ignoring her, looking around for friends, or for waiters serving champagne.

The humidity was annoying her too, the air so wet that you felt like you were breathing in globs of moisture instead of air. She looked up. Overhead fans turned lazily, moving the hot air from side to side, not bringing her any relief. Then, someone stepped on her feet. And that was it. The camel's back was broken. She had to get out of there.

She shoved her way impatiently through the tightly packed room, looking for the exit. She crossed the hallway with long steps. Giant mirrors with gilded frames on both sides of the hallway threw her image back at her. Her hair was dark and frizzy with moisture, her pretty concert outfit was rumpled and stuck to her body like glue. She looked away, horrified. She was getting to the age where it mattered what you looked like, especially when you had a mother as beautiful as Nicola. She hurried. She felt like something was behind those mirrors, watching her, following her, something that shouldn't be there. She picked up her steps.

She walked to the front of the hotel, leaving behind the heavy indoor air, leaving behind the oversweet scent of expensive perfume and bouquets of flowers, and the aroma of the food coming from the buffet tables.

She pushed the glass doors to the main entrance open and stepped outside. What a relief, to breathe in the fresh air of the outdoors. There was a soft wind that dried away the moisture on her upper lip and played briefly with her hair. She carefully balanced the crawfish boules and the meat pies in her hands as she walked. She was very pleased with herself that she had thought to pick up a few things from the buffet table. She was very hungry.

Leaving the concert hall had been a small act of rebellion. She had never stepped out on her own after a recital without letting someone know where she was going. But hey, her mother would be so busy being adored by everyone that she probably wouldn't miss her at all.

The warm, humid breeze brought her the salty scents of the sea, and tiny grains of sand found their way into her mouth settling between her teeth. The sun was going down, coloring the horizon yellows and pinks where the sky met the sea. She closed the doors behind her and all indoor noises ceased and were replaced by the quiet whoosh of the waves slithering on the golden yellow sand as they ebbed and then retreated. All of a sudden, a wave of white birds took off from the rocks to her right and flew away squawking into the clouds.

Margo walked down to the beach enjoying the solitude. She found a bench close to the water and sat down to eat her goodies, admire the boats bobbing on the water, and watch the people running around the beach, picking up their towels and their stuff before it got dark.

A tall young man appeared from behind some shrubs and sat down on the same long bench and all friendly, picked a conversation with her. He mentioned that there was a spot up on top of the salt cliff that was perfect for selfies, and he pointed to his right where the beach ended and a slight escarpment led to the top of a small hill. She should definitely go up there and take some pictures, he said, to capture the beauty of the Louisiana coast as a souvenir. Margo watched him as he got up and left, and decided to follow his suggestion. Why not? Assuming that there was plenty of time to get up there, take some pictures and hurry back before her mother missed her, Margo wiped her greasy hands on her pants and set out to explore the low-lying salt cliffs of Half Moon Bay.

She strolled along the beach, and she laughed when a frothy wave came all the way up to her feet and wet her shoes. The sudden feeling of independence was unexpectedly sweet, and she happily took a number of pictures with her cell phone while she climbed the gentle incline. Within minutes she was looking at the bay under her feet, watching it turn first into a million shades of reds and purples and then a more threatening tone of pewter. The beachgoers were gone, and the flocks of birds had all flown home. For a second it had been amazing to be up there, almost at the top of the world, almost as free as the birds themselves, letting the last rays of the sun warm her face, and the breeze play with her hair. But then she realized she had wasted too much time, and it had gotten almost dark.

The ledge where she was standing wasn't too narrow, so she turned her body carefully and began her descent back toward the beach. But just a few feet ahead, the ledge became unstable and began crumbling under her weight, sending dust and salt rocks into the void beneath. Startled by the sudden realization of danger, she cried out and stepped back. As she instinctively put her palms out against the dirt wall behind her, the cell phone slipped out of her hand. Her breath caught in her throat when she saw it flip in the air a couple of times before it smashed on the rocks below. A little piece of her heart broke. That cellphone had been a hard-earned reward for good behavior. It had been a sign of trust. Her mom would never forgive her, nor would she ever get her another one. She backtracked to a safe spot and stopped to catch her breath and quiet her heart.

She was in a pickle. Instead of walking all the way to the top of the cliff as she should have, she had chosen to take a lower path, a ledge about six feet under it. Now she realized it had been a dumb thing to do because she had nowhere to go. She looked up. The edge of the cliff wasn't high. If she turned around to face the wall and extended her arms, she could almost touch the clumps of weeds growing up there, but she would never manage to climb to the top on her own.

Without moving much, and with her heart beating so hard that she could barely hear herself think, she looked around and explored her options. The ledge kept on going sort of parallel to the cliff for a while and then disappeared into the darkness ahead. Should she risk keeping on going, without knowing where it would take her? Into the dark?

Margo stood deathly still, unable to make a decision. With sweaty hands, she held on to small tufts of grass sticking out of the dirt next to her, knowing well that they would never support her if she slipped. The tide was low, too. Sharp rocks—visible enough in the pale moonlight—stuck out of the water promising to crash her to bits if she fell. She was a good swimmer and would have risked jumping into the water since she was not so high up. But with those rocks down there? No way.

And then, all of a sudden, total night fell. And with the darkness came all those feelings of despair and regret. She wished she hadn't been so impatient. She wished she had followed the rules. She wished she had stayed in the recital hall, close to her mom. She wanted to take it all back. She was very scared. Tears rolled down her face as she made all kinds of promises to God and to all His Saints if only they would save her. But the minutes ticked away and no help was coming.

Once in a while the moon came out from behind layers of clouds and shone its pale moonlight on the restless sea making the tips of the waves shimmer like liquid silver. Thankful that at least it was a clear night, Margo stood still and waited. She had never been this scared in her short life.

Help, she screamed a few times, faintly, hopelessly, trying to be heard over the restless splashing of the surf. Maybe her mom would realize that she was gone and send a search party. But who was she kidding? Everyone was at the reception drinking, eating, having fun, and too busy to miss her. And without her cell phone, she was unable to let anyone know that she was in trouble.

The fog was coming up fast, and a sticky moisture filled the salty air and made it heavy, making it hard to breathe. She wiped the sweat sticking to her upper lip and the tears that wouldn't stop coming, blurring her vision. How long could she keep this up? She better think of something because her legs were going numb. She was too terrified to try to sit down and too terrified to keep walking. Finally, she gave up all hope. She was exhausted. She would have to stand there until her strength failed her and fall to her death, and days later the search party would find her floating to shore, nibbled to pieces by hungry fish. She sobbed inconsolably. Ugh, what a sad way to go.

Margo morbidly planned her own funeral. She imagined her mother—holding dozens of snow-white roses in her slender arms—crying for her with despair. It would be a fancy funeral. Everything her mom planned was always top-notch. Friends and family would gather in the local church, and the choir would sing *Panis Angelicus*. Everyone would cry.

She was already flinching from the spadefuls of dirt flung on her coffin when she heard a faint barking coming out of the heavy fog of her imagination. She paid attention and heard the bark again. Her throat was dry with thirst and fear, but she managed a weak help. Then, realizing that nobody was going to hear that simpering cry, she made an effort and began screaming. The barking got louder and louder, and before long it was on top of her head. She lifted her eyes toward the sound and by the pale moonlight saw a fawn-colored furry face with a long dribble of saliva looking down at her, panting.

"Are you still alive down there?" a man's voice asked.

"I think so, but I'm very scared. How did you find me?"

"It was Paco."

"Paco?"

"Yes, my dog Paco. He's hungry. We were going to have dinner after our evening stroll, but he sniffed the bench in front of the Pirate Bay Hotel and took off in a tear."

"I put the meat pies on the bench while I ate the crawfish boules."

"So that's how he picked up your scent. You probably still smell like fish. Dogs can pick up anything."

"It's my clothes. I wiped my hands on my pants. Can you help me up?"

"Wouldn't it be easier if you went back the way you came?"

"No, it wouldn't. The ledge gave way under my feet and crumbled. I'll fall to my death if I slip. I'm not going back that way. So can you help me up?"

"I think so. I could lower the dog's leash and pull you up."

"It won't work," Margo said, shaking her head, thinking about the sharp rocks and the dark waters under her feet. She was going to fall and crash, and the rocks were going to tear her to pieces. "It just won't work," she repeated despondently.

"And why not? Paco is a very big dog and he wears a thick leash and a powerful harness. We can do this."

"I'm scared." Her voice trembled and she clenched her hands to stop them from shaking.

"Of course you are. I am too, but I won't let you fall, I promise. I'm young and strong, and hopefully, you're short and skinny. It will work."

The dog Paco barked with enthusiasm as a long, sturdy-looking leash and harness descended to her reach. Margo stuck her right arm in the harness and wrapped the thick leash around her wrist.

"Is it a long leash?" she asked, trying not to sound terrified.

"It's long enough. Quit worrying. Paco and I will pull you up. It's only a few feet. No biggie."

Margo was slowly pulled up. Clinging to tufts of grass with her left hand, she stepped on jutting rocks and into narrow crevasses on the cliff wall pretending she was wall-climbing at the gym, and before she knew it, she was in the young man's arms. Paco the dog was excited beyond words. He whimpered and wagged his tail as if he had done all the pulling. Margo got on her knees and gave him a big hug wetting his fur with her tears. *Thank you for saving my life, Paco,* she whispered into his ears.

"What on earth were you doing down there?" the young man asked.

"Someone said this was a nice place to take pictures. It didn't sound dangerous. But I took the path instead of going all the way to the top of the cliff. And then it started getting dark, and when I tried to go back down, the path crumbled under my feet, and my cell phone fell into the water, and I didn't know what to do."

"How old are you anyway?"

"I'm fifteen."

"You should be old enough to know that cliff climbing in the late afternoon is very dangerous. You could have gotten yourself killed."

"I just wanted to go for a walk. My mom was busy with her fans at the homecoming reception, and I needed some fresh air. I don't know anyone here, and she's always surrounded by people, and I felt lonely, I guess. I don't know. I didn't think it was going to get dark so fast."

"Hey, I heard about that. It's that opera woman's homecoming. Are you the Fontaine girl?"

"Yes, I'm the Fontaine girl, Margo."

"Then nice to meet you, Margo Fontaine. My name is Jack Bernard, and this here is my dog, Paco. Welcome to Half Moon Bay." He gave her a friendly pat on her back. "Come on. Follow us. We'll take you back to the hotel."

Margo followed Jack and Paco along the trail. For a while, they walked under some trees, taking the long way back to town. It was too dark to see anything other than bits of the dog's light fur ahead and the back of Jack's shirt where slender rays of moonlight filtered through the branches, and they didn't talk much. It was a long walk—or at least it felt like it. Margo scampered after Jack and his dog, stumbling in the dark over clumps of vegetation and remnants of rocky buildings that Jack called the Old Town, what was left of it.

The darkness was full of strange noises and mysteriously deep moments of silence. Margo listened to the night in awe. Cicadas and frogs sang to the moon until you got close to them and then went quiet for a long, long time, as if they had never sung at all. Then, all you could hear were twigs and dry leaves crunching under your footsteps, echoing against the silence.

But beyond these noises, she thought she heard something else, something that sounded like an extra set of footsteps, something coming from behind her. She stopped and turned quickly, instinctively, toward the sound of footsteps, but just as suddenly they had stopped as well. She did see a shadow, or was it really a shadow, that moved quietly and hid behind a tree? Was someone following them? Or was it her imagination?

"Are you coming, Fontaine?" Jack asked her from way ahead and turned around without stopping. "Don't get lost now."

"Coming," she said and broke into a jog to catch up with them. But the moment was broken. The magic of Old Town was now scary, as if monsters were hiding behind the crumbling walls and the lone standing columns. There was something following them. She was absolutely sure.

Paco seemed to know his way well enough and barked once in a while to make sure he was still being followed. *We're coming*, Jack reassured him every time, and they continued on. Maybe Paco, too, sensed that there was something out there not quite right.

Soon, away in the distance, the lights of Half Moon Bay appeared from behind the dilapidated walls and the bushes of the Old Town, twinkling cheerfully. Jack hooked the leash to Paco's harness, and they crossed a number of busy streets. They were back among the honking cars and the street lights, and the laughter and conversation of the people strolling on the walkway by the beach.

Finally, Margo saw the neon lights of the Pirate Bay Hotel flashing colorful in the near distance. She could already hear the music coming from the reception. It sounded like popular opera excerpts—the chamber orchestra entertaining the beautiful people. She bet that her mom hadn't even noticed her absence.

Margo rushed toward the lights with relief. She suddenly felt thirsty, and hungry, and overwhelmed. She turned around and looked at Jack and tried to explain how grateful she was. But the words stuck in her throat.

"I know, Fontaine. You're welcome. You must have been very scared. I'm just glad we found you before you got hurt."

"I thought I was going to die. You saved my life." Margo stared at the young man, so handsome, so kind looking. His dark blond hair shone reddish and bluish under the Pirate Bay's neon lights. And at that moment Margo knew that she had just fallen in love.

"Your mom will be relieved to know that you're safe," Jack told her.

"Oh, she probably didn't even notice that I was gone, busy with all those people admiring her." She shrugged. She must have said that in a wistful tone because Jack quickly took her by the arms to reassure her.

"Listen, Fontaine, you'll be admired too when you're done growing up and you get rid of the braces and comb your hair. Give it some time." Then Jack laughed and the corners of his eyes wrinkled, and Margo smiled.

"Well, Jack and Paco, thank you for saving my life. I'll be forever grateful. Will I ever see you again?"

"Who knows? You'll take off to unknown lands with your mom, and Paco and I will go back to school, and the years will go by. But maybe we'll come across each other unexpectedly one day and won't even recognize each other."

"Not me. I'll never forget you." Margo smiled shyly at him.

"Then why don't we do this? Today is the 1st of June. Every year that we find ourselves in Half Moon Bay on this same exact date, let's come here and sit in the lobby of the Pirate Bay. Maybe that way we'll meet again." And Paco barked, and it all sounded so perfect, and Margo couldn't help but wonder at the amazing adventure she had had tonight.

She watched Jack and Paco saunter away. Paco's tail was still wagging wildly. It had been an exciting night for him as well. At the end of the path they both turned to look at her, and Jack waved for the last time. Her heart tightened as she waved back. She wondered if she would ever see them again.

As she turned around toward the hotel, she thought she saw a shadow move behind a tree. She squinted and looked carefully into the darkness but the shadow didn't move again. The neon lights were so bright that she could have been mistaken. But she shrugged. It didn't matter any longer. She was safe.

She pushed the glass door open and was momentarily disoriented by the bright lights shining in every chandelier and every lamp. It was as if all those hours of her being lost hadn't happened at all.

She crossed the empty lobby walking softly on the thick, richly tufted amber-colored carpeting. She followed the sounds of the party and looked around for her mother. Waiters in tuxes and bow ties glided smoothly among the guests bearing trays loaded with canapés or with flutes of champagne. People mingled, moved around, and laughed. Nobody realized she had been gone for hours.

The deep red velvet dress was visible miles away. There she was—the incomparable Fontaine—in a tight group of admirers, laughing, showing her perfect pearly teeth, her cheeks flushed, her eyes shiny. She looked ecstatic. She loved being surrounded by admirers. It was this and her love for the arts that made her life worth living.

Margo watched her happily for a few minutes, glad to be back in one piece, and then realized that something was off. Her mother had put on her elbow-length black satin gloves, and Margo suddenly found that disturbing, even though she couldn't say why. The gloves were always in Nicola Fontaine's purse but tucked into a pocket. Why would she have worn them on a hot, humid night like this one?

"She's a tough act to follow, isn't she?" a bitter voice told her. She turned around and saw that it was Ava Sigur who she hadn't noticed, sitting on a white leather sofa propped up by exotic pillows. The multicolored silk of the pillows gave some life to the unglamorous white satin dress and put some color into Ava Sigur's pale skin. She was holding an unlit cigarette at the end of an impossibly long filter.

"I thought you weren't supposed to smoke when you're a singer."

"It's not lighted. I don't really smoke anymore. But whenever I sing a duet with that woman, the stress makes me want to smoke again. You're the Fontaine kid, aren't you?"

"Yes. Margo Fontaine. I heard you sing. You're very good."

"And how would you know that, Margo Fontaine?" she asked in a sarcastic voice. "Aren't you too young to know about such things?"

"Maybe I'm young, but I've been around singers all my life. I can tell when someone's good."

"I'll have to take the compliment then. Do you sing as well?"

"Only occasionally. My voice is not as good as my mom's," she said, trying to forget how many times she had been asked the same question before.

"Nobody's is. Do you want to come sit and keep me company for a bit? Everyone else is busy with her, and I'm tired of sitting here all alone. I'll tell the *garçon* to bring you something to drink. You're about what, fourteen, fifteen?"

"Fifteen." Margo sat down primly next to Ava Sigur on the long white couch. Self-consciously, she brushed some burrs and small dead leaves off the hem of her slacks.

"Did you know that when your mother was your age she could already sing like a *rossignol*?"

"I've heard. I take voice lessons, but I'll never be as good as she is."

"Yes. I know what you mean."

Margo searched for her mother with her eyes and saw her in a corner talking to some man she had never seen before. The man—big, burly and shabbily dressed—looked angry, and Nicola did too, and he said something close to her ear, and she pushed the man away violently and walked away. But he grabbed her roughly by the arm and pulled her back to him. Margo, reacting instinctively to protect her mother, still pumped with the adrenaline of her adventure, jumped up from the couch and almost ran to where her mother was, pushing drunken guests out of her way, spilling drinks and stepping on elegant evening shoes as she went. Then she angrily got between them.

"Leave her alone," she told the big, burly stranger that up close looked more like a gangster than an opera lover. He smirked through dirty, yellow, tobacco-stained teeth, said something rude that Margo didn't quite understand, turned around, and left.

Nicola had gone white and was shaking in Margo's arms. She looked exhausted. There were deep, dark shadows under her eyes, and her lipstick was smudged as if someone had tried to kiss her by force. Margo shuddered with anger. She looked around but didn't see the guy again. Nobody seemed to have noticed the confrontation. She pulled her mother protectively toward the elevators and told her it was time to go. She had already had too much to drink. In so many ways her mother was fragile and vulnerable like a child, and she—the child—had to do the mothering, especially after concerts or recitals when her mother became too tired or too tipsy to think.

Nobody noticed when they left the party. At least nobody tried to stop them. When she stepped into the elevator, she felt hostile eyes on her back and turned around quickly to see who it was, but she must have been mistaken because there was no one there. With a quiet whizz, the elevator doors closed on them, and soon she forgot all about it.

And suddenly, in the blink of an eye, here she was again—five years later, five years to the day—sitting on the same white leather sofa in the Pirate Bay lobby, trying to figure out where all those years had gone.

Chapter 1

Monday, June 1st

MARGO LOOKED AT HER WATCH with mounting anxiety and bit back the urge to pace. He's not coming, she thought. Every year on June the 1st since she'd learned how to drive, she had faithfully come back to Half Moon Bay to keep her rendezvous with Jack, sitting for hours in the lobby of the Pirate Bay Hotel, hoping to see him again. Yet she had gone away disappointed every single time. Why did she keep doing this to herself?

She put the magazine back on the table and got up from the white leather sofa she had just spent two hours sitting on. She looked around self-consciously, wondering if anyone had noticed that she had been stood up again, and she smoothed down her skirt. It wasn't like she really expected Jack to show up to their yearly date, or anything.

She crossed the Hallway of Mirrors that had intimidated her so much when she was younger. The hotel had been renovated and expanded in the last few years, but they never touched anything in the Hallway of Mirrors. Eleven huge mirrors, incredibly old, every one with a different carved and gilded frame, five on one side, six on the other, with a burnished patina, and a dulled power of reflection. Why eleven? Would it have killed them to add one or take one away? The original flooring had also been kept. The herringbone wooden parquet began and ended with the hallway, creaky, unpolished, tooled out of the remains of a brigantine that the early inhabitants of the bay had enticed to safety during a storm to murder the travelers and rob them of their cargo. Nasty story. She wished it wasn't true.

And then, those mirrors. She'd heard that they were an inheritance from way back when the place was first built. There was a legend connected to them, to the mirrors. Sir Henry Morgan—otherwise known as Morgan the Pirate—was the ruthless 17th-century legendary Welsh pirate who raided the Spanish settlements of the Caribbean. And that was not all he raided. He left behind an army of redheaded babies, born in every port city nine months after his departure, to the embarrassment of so many married women. Of course, there was no point in denying the father. Most of the indigenous inhabitants of his ports of call had never seen a redhead in their lives.

After helping to write the Code of the Pirate Brethren and being knighted by Charles II of England, he was appointed lieutenant-governor of Jamaica. Sometime during these years, he took up the study of alchemy and vanished from history for a while, discovering the secret to immortality, it was said, and becoming known as the Shadow Lord. Anyway, somehow these mirrors were connected to Sir Morgan and his shadowy pursuits. Wagging tongues swore that he began imprisoning the souls of his enemies into the mirrors. Not that she wanted to know, nor was anyone telling. Her aunts always bragged about Sir Morgan's stay in Half Moon Bay and the two locks of red hair that appeared in every Fontaine's hair at birth ever since, but that was all she knew. The point was, nobody dared touch the Hallway of Mirrors.

She walked the long hallway with a self-imposed confidence, pretending not to look at herself. How creepy: mirrors facing each other. She could almost feel eyes watching her from the other side. Had they not heard that mirrors facing each other could open a portal for evil entities to pass through?

She shrugged the uncomfortable feeling off and hurried on. All that rush to get here, all for nothing. Turning school papers in early, and all the begging and groveling, to be allowed to take tests ahead of time so she could hit the road and get back to Half Moon Bay. But she just couldn't stop herself. Ugh. As soon as June 1st started getting closer, Margo began the arduous job of talking herself into showing up. Never mind that the day before she had promised herself she wasn't coming. Promises, promises. Like Ulysses, she should have tied herself to the mast of common sense and personal pride to avoid being lured by the thought of seeing Jack. But at least Ulysses got the satisfaction of hearing the sirens sing, whereas she left empty-handed, every single time. It was just pitiful. It was embarrassing. Well, it was time to regain some personal dignity. This was going to be the very last time. It was a promise. It really was.

She stepped into the restaurant with relief, welcoming the modern open space of polished chrome and white Formica. Seemed like Mimi really liked white, she chuckled. And there was her favorite table by the big window, empty, waiting for her. The sun shone brightly on the waters of the scenic bay, making the tips of the waves shimmer. It was the beginning of tourist season and beach chairs and oversized umbrellas jostled for space on the narrow strip of sand even though the water wasn't quite yet warm enough to go in. She laughed softly. It was hard to remain grumpy when the weather was so pretty.

Half Moon Bay was a relatively small town, yet the Pirate Bay's restaurant was always full, and you were lucky if you could get a good table by the scenic windows. She waved to Manuel—the waiter—and asked for a café au lait.

"He didn't show?"

"No, Manuel, he didn't. This is the last time I wait for him."

"That's what you said last year."

"I did, didn't I?" Margo laughed a small self-conscious laugh. "But this time it's for real."

"Don't worry," Manuel told her. "If he comes in later, I'll tell him you were looking for him."

"Oh, no, please don't do that. Promise me you won't, and bring me some beignets as well. I need comfort food."

While she waited for her coffee and beignets, she watched expectantly the people come and go—still hoping that Jack would show last minute—while she did some quick thinking.

Margo put aside the letter that Manuel had just handed her and bit into a beignet. Relief ran through her body. Nobody made beignets like the cooks at the Pirate Bay. She was picking Jenny and her cats up at the bus station first thing in the morning. There were no rooms available anywhere in Half Moon Bay, not with the Regatta coming Sunday week. So her original idea was going to have to do. She poured some coffee and milk into the white-and-roses porcelain cup and stirred the sugar in absentmindedly. Jenny would have to spend the first couple of weeks of the summer hiding in the attic with her. It wouldn't be so bad. They could make it fun. Her great aunts were so old and so deaf that they would never figure out there was a stowaway upstairs. Not that there was anything wrong with having a friend over for the summer, but Margo felt a terrible apprehension, especially about the cats. As far as she knew, the aunts hated cats. It was best if they didn't find out.

She sipped her coffee for a while, doing her best not to look at the letter. After all, she recognized the handwriting, so what was in it was probably more of the same. She popped another beignet in her mouth. Strange how life had its twists and turns. Five years ago, she had watched her mom, at the height of her career, cast her spell over the inhabitants of Half Moon Bay. Two years later she was back, this time bringing her mom in a casket, to be buried in the family vault. Margo pushed away the sad memories and licked the powdered sugar off her fingers. She had always had a complicated relationship with her mom, who seemed more interested in her art and her admirers than in being a mother.

She watched the colorful boats bobbing on the water and sighed with longing, not quite knowing why. She picked up the letter and turned it around in her hand. She didn't want to open it. She really didn't. Until the night of the recital—the night that she had gotten lost and was saved by Jack and his dog Paco—she had never even set a foot in this town where her mother was born and raised. Even today, after having come back numerous times, she still felt like a stranger. An outsider. She stared at the letter, remembering how much fear and sorrow the others had brought her in the past, and she just wanted to cry. Time to go home.

Margo left a twenty by the coffee pot and got up. Although she had been coming back regularly to spend holidays with her aging aunts, she had never really felt wanted by them. Maybe Aunt Tilly had mellowed some, but Aunt Beth was a terror. Why did they keep asking her to come spend summers and Christmases with them? And if she knew they were not so fond of her, why did she keep accepting? In the end, why not, she reasoned, since she didn't have anywhere else to go anyway. They were all the family she had left, and there was always the hope that next time they'd be nicer to her.

She drove along Gulf Bay Boulevard, turned right on Saltwater Dr., and took a left on East Albatross. There, on the corner, much taller and much older than the other houses around it was the rambling mansion that the family had pretentiously named *The Hornet's Nest*. It was an Italianate style double-galleried mansion, although it couldn't be called a mansion anymore. It had once been a faded rose color, probably magnificent, with black ornate cast iron balustraded balconies and wide, overhanging eaves with brackets and cornices, but now the faded rose was dark with dirt and mildew, and the black paint was peeling off the balustrades.

She parked at the back of the house under a shady tree—by the wooden fence covered in a profusion of white and yellow jasmine—and inhaled the sweet citrusy scent that pervaded the whole back of the house.

In spite of the disappointment, the moment was perfect. The afternoon sky was blue and clear. The breeze carried the warm, salty air in from the sea and ruffled the flowers of the jasmine vine and the tiny bees that were always buzzing around it. She closed her eyes gratefully for a second and enjoyed the peace. Then, she walked carefully toward the house, struggling to avoid the tufts of weeds pushing up the uneven paving stones that threatened to sprain an ankle or break the heels off her shoes.

Through the back entrance, she smuggled upstairs several loads of shopping bags including cat food and cat litter. She placed the unopened letter in an old tin box, next to all the others. Then she quickly changed for dinner.

Chapter 2

The Dinner Party

STRANDED IN THE PAST, aunts Beth and Tilly still wore formal attire for evening meals. They favored outdated black taffeta dresses with high necks and few frills. Most of their outfits were faded and threadbare, but they didn't seem to notice. Their hairs were always gathered up on top of their head in chignons with loose, soft curls as if they were young women. It you were not used to it, it was a depressing sight.

Not that her own gown was in much better shape. She had found a handful of her mother's concert dresses up in the attic, and she had adapted them to her own body—needle and thread, and pinpricked fingers. Some had to be mended quite extensively. The lace outer layer of the deep red silk chiffon dress that she had on tonight had been almost impossible to mend. Up in the attic, the chest had been full of roaches and silverfish, ugh, and the clothes were full of holes. But she made the mistake of showing up to dinner in jeans only once. And she was never doing that again. Now, she looked just as depressing as the aunts—with her mended gown—but at least she was properly dressed.

She heard the first gong and hurried downstairs. The family was already gathered in the sitting room. She slowed down to enter the room with dignity and looked around. Cousin Robert turned toward her and sneered. He always wore the same white tie dinner outfit, but as he got heavier every time she saw him, it didn't much fit him anymore. If he had too much watercress soup tonight, those buttons would be sure to burst on his voluminous belly and go pop. *Bad Margo*, she scolded herself. *Be nice.*

Madeline, Robert's angry wife was sipping her sherry with a frown on her face. She barely looked up to say hello. There was tension in the air, and an absolute silence, and Margo had the feeling that the family had been arguing again. Father Armand—trying to be inconspicuous—stood to the side, pretending to be somewhere else. At least that was the way he looked.

Oh, goodie, Margo thought. Another fight. She accepted a sherry from a white-gloved Snail and went and mingled. Some Mozart concerto on the record player provided a civilized—if scratchy—background music to an otherwise uncomfortable moment. Then suddenly, everyone started talking at the same time.

After the second gong, Snail, their sour-faced butler served dinner in the formal dining room with the help of two local girls awkwardly wearing black uniforms with a starched lacy white pinny. On Sundays, they ate from the good china, on weekdays from the second-best. Wine was always served with meals, an endless supply of which had been collected by Grand-père François, the patriarch of the family.

It was a mercy that they ate by candlelight because the dining room was in such a state of decay. The white damask tablecloth wasn't really white any longer. Stubborn yellow stains and badly mended tears didn't take away from the dignity of the occasion, though. And newcomer guests, as was Father Armand, pretended that nothing out of ordinary was taking place, even though the occasion felt as if they were all playing parts in a comedy of ghosts long dead, feasting the living.

Aunt Beth was an expert in the art of genteel conversation and did her best to entertain a startled Father Armand. Meantime, Aunt Tilly, Cousin Robert, and Madeline sat stony-faced ignoring the three young ruffians who—immune to Aunt Beth's dragon stare—were destroying what was left of the dining room. Nobody seemed to do justice to the fabulous meal but her, barely nibbling on what was in front of them. It was a crime, too, because the *Boeuf Bourguignon* with the French-cut Green Beans was fabulous, and the Raspberry Meringue Mousse was to die for.

THE BURNING FIRE OF GREED

That night, the night before Jenny came to spend the summer, and Father Armand came to dinner for the first time with the family, a terrible storm passed by. They were sipping on their after-dinner Orange Curaçaos when suddenly the first lightning hit, making the chandeliers sway and the lights flicker. It felt as if an evil presence had moved through the house, touching with its tainted fingers everything and everyone, but nobody except Margo seemed to feel it. A second burst of lightning brightened the skies, and it seemed for a second that the stained glass windows on the top of the hallway stairs would burst and shatter into a million pieces, and an unbearable feeling of foreboding tore through Margo's heart. But within a few minutes, the storm blew out to sea. And yet, Margo couldn't shake off that ugly feeling inside her.

Cousin Robert was a regular in the house on East Albatross as he was there at least twice, three times a week. He often came to dinner with his family, especially on Sundays after Mass. Even though he was unfriendly and rather pretentious, the aunts loved him and fawned all over him. Robert—in return—bossed the aunts and their servants about like an autocrat, every bit the man of the house and the king of his kingdom. It was very unpleasant.

Margo didn't much care for Cousin Robert or his family. She tried to be charitable and have kind thoughts for them, but so few came to mind. The three boys kicked and pinched each other constantly, and the parents never corrected them. The wife, Madeline, was an uptight and unhappy creature that rarely took part in any conversation except to complain about the food, the wine, the temperature in the room, or Margo's presence.

Once dinner was over, the inevitable came next. "Do sing something for us," Aunt Beth or Aunt Tilly would say, and Margo would feel compelled to deliver an underwhelming rendition of some old fashioned song for Alto and Piano. Afterward, little snide comments would be made about her lack of artistic abilities. Even though it was something she was used to, it still rankled to always be compared to her mother.

But Robert did have one redeeming quality after all, she had to admit. He was a wonderful pianist and a pretty good singer. Love of music definitely ran in the family. While the aunts and the wife had their second or third glass of Curaçao, Robert would plop himself on the rickety piano bench and rifle through the sheet music on the stand.

"How about some Schubert tonight, Margo?" he would ask, and tear into a fabulous rendition of songs of love and loss. Their voices—Robert's Tenor and Margo's Alto—sounded wonderfully harmonious together, and these were the moments when Margo absolutely loved being part of a family and having a cousin who loved music as much as she did.

That night, that last night before Jenny's arrival, Robert surprised them with a stack of mildewed and disintegrating sheet music.

"I found them at a garage sale," he told her. "Look: Cole Porter. There's some other stuff as well, but let's try the Cole Porter tonight."

"I've never sung any of that," she told him self-consciously.

"Oh, don't worry. They all come with separate Alto sheet music. We're in luck. Now don't sulk, Margo. You'll love it."

Like a lamb led to slaughter, Margo took her position by the Bösendorfer. Robert quickly ran through the music, getting used to the unfamiliar chords and the melody. Meantime, Margo looked around. Aunts Beth and Tilly sat in one corner of the tattered Aubusson rug in their usual matching threadbare needlepoint chairs and gossiped in a soft monotone. Father Armand, having been roped into this impromptu recital, sat stiffly perched in an old armchair, close to the whispering aunts. You could tell that he was trying hard not to look at the faded portraits of the long-forgotten ancestors and the moth-eaten damask curtains, or the spider webs in the dark corners of the ceiling, or the peeling wallpaper around him. Poor Father Armand looked like he wanted to go home

Madeline, the malcontent wife, sat in another corner all by herself and watched her three horrid boys entertain themselves by pulling photographs out of an old album and tearing them into tiny pieces. It's none of my business, Margo told herself, controlling the urge to take the precious family memento out of their hands. If they don't mind, why should I?

Then Margo looked at Robert who nodded at her, and the music-making began. His tempo was rather slow for her taste, so she pretended she was Ella Fitzgerald and sang in a deep, old-fashioned sultry voice *Let's do it, let's fall in love.* She thought about Jack and his smile under the moonlight, and how she kept hoping to meet him again, and that childish infatuation with the handsome young man who had saved her life. Afterward, they sang the duet *Let's Misbehave.* Despite her dislike for Robert, she enjoyed these musical evenings tremendously, and she often wished that they would never end.

Then she bent down and picked up a folded piece of paper that had fallen out of the pack of sheet music. She held her breath in panic. It was just a to-do list, nothing more. But the handwriting was familiar. She had seen it before.

Chapter 3

Mrs. Cook Considers

ROSA NESTA TOOK ONE LOOK at the messy kitchen and felt like bolting. I'm getting a c*old in the mole* and nobody cares. Mrs. Cook this, and Mrs. Cook that. They treat me like a slave. They think that because my skin is darker than their uptight white, I can be treated like one. *Jessum Peace*, it will take me half the night to clean up this mess.

Rosa Nesta grumbled to herself as she walked back and forth from the dining room bringing in the dirty dishes. Then she pulled the broomstick from the closet behind the refrigerator and set about to sweep under the table.

There had been a time when she was grateful for this job. Young, freshly arrived from Jamaica, running away from an abusive and unfulfilling family life, she had thought cooking for a small family the stuff that dreams are made of. A well-paid job with a pretty room all her own that she could decorate whichever way she wanted, and plenty of money to buy quality clothes and shoes. And the master was nice to her. None of that getting drunk and running around the house after her, trying to pinch her behind. Oh no, the master was a good man, a Christian man. And whenever anyone tried to tell her that he was a womanizing rascal, she would say, "I don't believe you. My Monsieur François is a gentleman, and he would never do anything like that."

But much water had run under that bridge, and now Monsieur François was dead, and what he had left behind was not so pretty, no, no. Old Aunt Tilly was sort of nice sometimes, but that harridan of a woman, that Aunt Beth, well, she had been working for them for all of her life, and still she was scared of the woman.

Once she was done sweeping, she put a hand on a hip, stared at the wrinkled envelope under the dining table, and wondered if she should make an effort and bend down to get it. The years hadn't been kind to her body. She loved to eat and drink too much and was now vastly overweight. Bending down would take an enormous effort, and had the letter been under anyone else's seat, she would have just left it right where she had found it. But she couldn't let it go. She looked behind her shoulder to make sure that she was alone and poked at the envelope with the broom until it was within her reach. Then she painstakingly bent down to retrieve it and quickly put it in her crawfish patterned apron pocket. There would be plenty of time later, to read it in the privacy of her own room.

Chapter 4
The Regatta

THE HALF MOON BAY REGATTA was *the* yearly event that everyone who was someone had to attend. The festivities leading up to it lasted two whole weeks, in which market tents with souvenirs and local foods sprung up all over the place to the delight of the locals and the tourists alike. The first Regatta had consisted of barely a handful of local sailboats, but Brett Duval and the rest of the Yacht Club Regatta Committee had worked hard down the years to turn the race into an international event to benefit not only them but the whole community. Local vendors prepared for weeks in advance, cooking, making, baking, you name it, to benefit from the onslaught of tourists. Because of this, Brett Duvall knew he would never be replaced as president of the Yacht Club. The whole town adored him.

Up in the attic, Margo, swept up in the excitement, smiled. She and Jenny pulled an old chest to the narrow window and stood on it, side by side on their tiptoes, watching the preparations by the seashore through a pair of old binoculars. Up on a gentle incline, the attic of the house on East Albatross was high enough that they had an almost complete view of the bay over the weather-beaten rooftops of the smaller houses between them and the beach.

Already a long line of multicolored sailboats had arrived from marinas all over the east coast and parts of Europe and was anchored randomly in the relatively small bay, happily bobbing on the choppy waters. On the Boardwalk, dozens of people holding children by their hands and dogs by their leashes watched the construction of the bleachers that—Mardi Gras parade-style—would allow the town and its visitors to watch the festivities and the race.

Recognizable by his signature purple plaid shorts and purple visor, Brett Duval hurried from one stand to the other, checking personally on the progress of the builders. He was proud to say that the crowds would all get to come and watch the races for free. The Regatta was his gift to the town.

"That's Brett Duval, the one with the shiny bald head and aviator glasses," Margo told Jenny, passing her the binoculars. "He'll be the one to open the ceremonies tonight at the Grand Regatta Ball."

"How are we going to sneak out?"

"Easy, you'll see. We'll wait for Robert to come and pick the aunts up, and we'll have the house to ourselves. The Yacht Club is within walking distance—kind of—and we'll bring our party clothes in a bag, and we'll change in the bathrooms."

"Will they let us in?"

"I'm a Fontaine, Jenny. Of course, they'll let us in."

"And do we have to walk? Couldn't we drive?" Jenny asked.

"We could, but I'm afraid there won't be any parking left. Even if we took a taxi we would have to walk part of the way. The whole Boardwalk and the neighboring streets will all be closed to vehicles. But I promise you that it's not far."

"I hate to be here behind your family's back," Jenny said with her big sad eyes looking at her feet.

"I know, Jenny. I wish I was brave enough to tell them the truth. If it was just you, I would, really. But it's too late now anyway. You're already here. If I told them now, I have a feeling that they would be angry at me."

"But why would they?"

"I don't know, Jenny. Because I didn't ask for permission. Besides, they hate cats. What would we do if they kicked the cats out?"

"Would they?"

"I don't know about Aunt Tilly. She's kind of nice. But I'm scared of Aunt Beth."

"Then why do you even bother spending the summers here?"

"Ugh, I got roped into it. And then I sort of became fond of Aunt Tilly. She always looks so lost. It makes me want to take care of her. Besides, I have nowhere else to go."

"Yeah, me either," Jenny added sadly. "I sent my aunt a postcard before I left school so she would know where I was spending the summer, but I don't think she cares." She was pretty much in the same boat as Margo. After her uncle and protector died, his young wife—the new one—told Jenny to make sure and never come back to spend school holidays with her and the kids. She was going to have to grow up and find a life of her own. "Thanks for taking us in, Margo. The cats and I would be homeless for the summer without you."

"You'll never be homeless as long as you have me. Next time we'll plan better. We could rent a house close to school, and then we wouldn't have to leave after the semester. And that reminds me… If we don't get these cats some chicken, they'll tear the attic door down." Jenny laughed and followed her out of the attic. "I can smell the chicken too."

The girls snuck quietly down the back stairs. The house was as quiet as a mausoleum. Over the perennial smell of mildew, an all-pervading layer of dust covered every inch of the unused back stairwell and the attics. The creaky back stairs, once used exclusively by slaves and servants so that they would remain invisible to the eyes of the owners, were utilitarian, unfinished, and badly lit. Back there, even in the middle of a sunny day, it was as dark as if it was night time already. And if you put your ear to the wood, you could hear the roaches rustling blindly in the hollow walls, agitating their paper-like wings as they rubbed against each other. And that's why, she told Jenny, it was best not to have too much light. Because you don't want to know what lurks in the shadows.

"Why the attic," Jenny asked. "Didn't they offer you one of the rooms downstairs?"

"At the beginning, there was talk of that. Aunt Tilly got very excited and mentioned that she wanted me in the room next to hers. But as soon as Aunt Tilly said the words, Aunt Beth slammed her fist on the table and said no way, and over her dead body. So I suspect that whatever

Aunt Tilly wants, Aunt Beth shoots down. To avoid the bickering, I offered to stay in the attic. Aunt Beth loved that."

"Your aunt Beth is a bully. I don't understand why they even want you here."

"To tell you the truth, I don't either."

The girls had arrived at the kitchen door, and Margo pushed it open carefully and peeked inside. There on the butcher table sat a lovely plate of lunch leftovers.

"Hey look, Jenny, there's Jerk Chicken left, and cabbage salad and fried rice. Yummy. I might have to eat lunch again. We'll bring the cats some of the chicken."

Meantime, Rosa Nesta had snuck up on them and gave them a gruff *ejem*.

"*Me back foot!* I knew it," she said triumphantly. "I hear sounds at night and I think I'm imagining them. But my hearing is very good. And then I hear you, Miss Margo, talking to yourself, and I wonder why a *jubee* like you would talk to herself for hours and hours."

"Oh, Mrs. Cook, we didn't hear you coming in."

"But I hear you sneaking down the stairs. I hear two sets of footsteps and I think to myself, but how is that possible? There's nobody else in the house. Or is there? And finally today I decide to quit being scared of funny noises and come to see for myself what is going on."

"Please don't tell on us, Mrs. Cook. This is my friend Jenny from school. She and her cats had nowhere to go because her uncle died and her aunt kicked her out of the house. She told Jenny she had to grow up and find her own path in life. But Jenny isn't ready for that, at least not right now. It all happened too suddenly."

"Well, at least I know I am not going bananas," said Rosa Nesta with her hands on her voluminous hips. "Since you're here already, you might as well eat. So tell me, how long have you been hiding upstairs, Miss Jenny? And are you the one eating all my leftovers?"

"Jenny," said Margo, "Mrs. Cook has lived in this house for like fifty years now. She knew my mom, didn't you, Mrs. Cook?"

"I sure did. Miss Nicole was the prettiest little girl I had seen in my entire life. Much prettier than her older sisters Miss Beth and Miss Tilly. And Monsieur François her daddy adored her, so he gave her everything she ever wanted, and she grew up to be spoiled and arrogant. Even to me, she was sometimes mean. To me who had helped care for her since the day she was born," she said with a sigh. "Then she realized how talented she was and started calling herself Nicola Fontaine because it sounded more operatic. And then she became famous and we never saw her again."

"How about my dad? Did you ever meet him?" Margo asked between mouthfuls of fried rice.

"I swore many years ago I would never mention that man or his name under this roof and I'm not going to get started now."

"But I have a right to know, Mrs. Cook. Who else am I going to ask?"

"That I can't help you with, *sweetness*. You better leave your past alone. In this house, with this family, you better *watchya* back. These are people who say they love you and then don't hesitate to *skank* you. And now eat up and go away so I can finish cleaning up this kitchen. Me feet are swollen and I need to put them up. Oh, and don't forget the chicken for the cats."

Rosa Nesta adjusted the colorful cloth band than kept her wild curly hair under control and left the kitchen.

"I wonder what she meant when she said watchya back," Jenny said.

"Yeah, and I wonder what it means to skank someone."

Chapter 5

Someone Tries To Kill Margo

THE SUN FINALLY WENT DOWN in a spectacular blaze of colors, and the stars came out and filled the dark blue sky. Margo got on her tiptoes and took one quick look at the darkening town before closing the high attic window. The sailing ships that dotted the bay were decked out with festive, twinkling, multicolored lights, and down at the Yacht Club, all lights were on. A long line of car headlights came in and out of focus as passengers were driven to the main door to be dropped off, and their cars were taken away by their chauffeurs to be parked out back.

The Louisiana air was heavy and humid as usual, buzzing with mosquitoes and Sphinx moths, and it carried the beating bass notes of music all the way to the attic and through the windows where the girls were getting ready. When they decided they couldn't wait any longer, they made sure the cats had enough food and water. Then, they carefully closed the attic door behind them and crept downstairs.

The house was quiet. Without the constant clop-clop of Aunt Beth's walking stick and Rosa Nesta's radio always on in the kitchen, the house suddenly felt heavy, abandoned. The aunts had decided to forego their formal dinner at home in favor of the more exciting high-end buffet at the Yacht Club, which gave Mrs. Cook, Snail, and the young maids the night off. They were probably out there by the beach already, enjoying the cookouts the community had organized for the town folks. Once outside, they giggled and set off toward the Yacht Club.

"Didn't the aunts ask you to the Ball?" Jenny asked.

"Initially, yes. They wanted me to go with a friend of Robert's who's looking for a wife. But I said no thanks, I'd rather stay home. If he's anything like my cousin, I definitely don't want to go out with him. And I'm not looking for a husband."

"Are you still hoping to see Jack again?"

"No. Of course not. That was just childish infatuation. I'm not planning on spending another June the 1st sitting in the Pirate Bay lobby waiting for him ever again."

"You say that every year."

"I know. But this time I mean it."

The girls crossed Salt Water and turned right on Sky Harbor Boulevard. You could smell the excitement in the air. The high school band—to compete with the circus loop-music of the carousel—was belting out a well-known Sousa march down by the waterfront, and Margo found herself subconsciously matching her footsteps to the contagious beat. When she realized what she was doing, she blushed in the dark and laughed.

Every house's front lights were on. Colorful flags had been hung on the light posts on the Boulevard, and these flapped cheerfully in the wind. Young men drove by in *voitures décapotables* and honked and whistled at groups of dolled-up girls walking together toward the beach. The crepe myrtles were in their full glory, and sudden gusts of wind tore off fragile pink and purple blooms that floated about gracefully in the air before they fell.

Down on the Boardwalk—which ran parallel to the waterfront—car access had been shut down from Old Town on the south side all the way to the Yacht Club. Dozens of multicolored striped tents dotted the edge of the walkway and sold everything from team t-shirts and memorabilia to Creole meat pies and cotton candy. Not that the fun-loving people of South Louisiana needed an excuse to party, no. Just start counting all the festivities in their calendar: the Boudin Festival, the Crawfish Festival, the Shrimp Festival, the International Festival, Mardi Gras, etc., etc. The list went on and on. And every one of these events was a good excuse to gather and dance a waltz or a two-step to the tunes of the local Cajun bands, and eat boudin and meat pies and drink beer 'till you dropped.

Further down, Margo and Jenny stopped to observe the French sailing team dressed in their blue, white, and red off-water uniform jerseys trying to converse in French with some of the local Cajuns. It wasn't going well. It was almost as if they were speaking two different languages and had resorted to hand gestures to make themselves understood.

"Formal ties between Louisiana and France were severed over two centuries ago," Margo explained to Jenny, "so their idiomatic expressions and slang have become vastly different from each other. It's like hearing an old French dialect spoken with a modern American accent."

A few steps further down, they stopped to let a group of noisy kids pass in front of them, and it was then that Margo looked up and noticed that something at the edge of her vision had begun to move in the wrong direction. A battered jeep had quietly detached itself from the long line of parked cars on Sky Harbor Boulevard, and instead of turning right at the wooden horses that separated the crowd walking on the Boardwalk from the vehicles, it headed straight their way. But at that point, Margo didn't react.

All of a sudden, mayhem erupted. A woman's horrified scream pierced the night. Soon, other people were joining in, yelling at each other to get out of the way. Women scrambled to pick their children up, and men jumped out of the way as the renegade jeep ran down the wooden horses that kept the cars from the Boardwalk and jumped the curb, heading steadily in the direction of the oblivious girls who were still standing close to the French team, staring horrified at what was going on, but still not moving to get out of the way.

It all happened in the blink of an eye. While onlookers stared in horror at the jeep careening straight toward the two girls frozen in their spots like deer in the headlights, the Frenchmen woke from their stupor and started running toward Margo and her friend. They waved their arms and yelled warnings, trying to tell the girls in broken English that they were in danger. Margo turned around to look first at the young men running toward them and then toward the jeep and saw that it was a mere dozen feet away when she finally reacted. She grabbed Jenny's arm and pulled her, but it was too late. The jeep had picked up some speed and lurched toward them bumping over scattered souvenirs and toys as people hurried to get out of its way. It seemed like Margo and Jenny would never make it out of harm's way when two of the Frenchmen—who had decided it was worth risking their lives to save a couple of pretty girls—ran toward them and reached them in the nick of time. They threw themselves heroically against the girls, just like in the movies, pushing them out of the jeep's murderous path, and they all landed in a startled heap on a strip of grass, safely out of harm's way. Meantime, the jeep never stopped. By the time they got up from the ground and dusted themselves off, there was no trace of it anywhere.

They stared at each other surprised, and one of the young men asked, "What have you two *demoiselles* done, that someone just tried to kill you?"

Margo quickly looked around. The jeep had left a swath of destruction as the driver rammed on, and some children were still crying, but nobody seemed to have gotten hurt.

Accompanied by the Frenchmen who had probably saved their lives, Margo and Jenny gathered their belongings from the floor and headed to the Yacht Club, silent and overwhelmed by what had just happened. Soon the people—who had gathered in startled groups to discuss the horrifying event—returned to normal, and it dawned on Margo that even though she and Jenny had just almost died, life around them hadn't missed a beat. It was a sobering thought.

As they got closer to the club with their new friends, they left behind the Sousa March that the high schoolers were still belting out. Little by little Margo's heartbeats returned to normal and she discreetly dried her sweating palms on her clothes. Whatever had prompted the driver of the jeep to career madly in their direction, it had been an accident because there was no reason to believe that he had intended to hurt them, as the young Frenchman had hinted. And yet, you just never knew.

THE BURNING FIRE OF GREED

In the marina, welcoming multicolored lights blinked in the darkness, reflected in the water, making the bay shimmer like a jeweled crown, blending with the shine of the stars in the sky. The air was warm and salty, and a pleasant breeze played with Margo's hair and with the leaves of the bushes around her. The young man who had saved her and had offered his arm was handsome and friendly, and she soon forgot what had just happened. Once she and Jenny changed into their party clothes, they sat with their new friends at a quiet table behind a column and determined to have fun.

Until—that is—she heard her name, mentioned by a familiar voice. And what she heard made a cold shiver run through her body, as if someone had just walked over her grave.

Chapter 6
Aunt Tilly Says Too Much

"OH, BETH, YOU SHOULD LEAVE that poor Margo alone. She's such a nice girl, and she's never done you any harm."

"Just her existence has caused me harm, Tilly. I can't even stand to look at her. Don't you understand?"

"No, I don't. Robert already has everything he wants. And you know papa would be very displeased."

"Well, papa is long gone and buried, so his opinion would be of no consequence."

"Oh, Beth, you shouldn't be so cruel."

"And you should shut up. Here comes Robert."

Margo peeked from behind the column. Neither Margo nor her aunts had realized they were sitting so close together. While her friends chatted, she slowly inched her chair closer to the adjoining table.

She followed Aunt Beth's gaze and saw that Cousin Robert and his sour-faced wife Madeline had just entered the room. Robert looked uncomfortable in his tux. He tugged at his bow tie repeatedly as he looked around frowning, searching for the aunts. With one hand, he possessively pulled his wife along, who took awkward little steps in her high-heeled shoes to keep up with him. She wore a glorious green silk evening gown that hung on her inelegantly because she was so extremely slender. Robert pulled out chairs for them and sat down.

"Hello ladies," he said unpleasantly. "You two look like you were arguing. Is everything all right, or is little Margo causing trouble again?"

"Your little cousin as you call her could cause you a world of trouble if she ever found out the truth," Beth said.

"I think you should tell her the truth Beth," Tilly kept insisting. "This is just not fair."

"What I don't think is fair" chimed in Robert's wife "is that she should be invited down every school holiday. Nobody enjoys her company, and she doesn't belong in polite company. She was raised like a wild child with all that homeschooling and lack of discipline."

"Don't say that, Madeline," Aunt Tilly cut in. "She's a good girl. She's smart, and she's going to college to better herself, and what's more important is that she has a kind heart."

"And how would you know about that?" Beth cut in.

"She's always been kind to me. I vote that we tell her the truth."

"You don't get to vote."

"Then I will tell her myself. We are her family, and we ought to take care of her, not take advantage of her," insisted Tilly.

Margo listened intently, but the rest of the conversation got cut off when the orchestra began to play. She moved closer, and then a little closer, but the music kept getting louder, and the rest of the conversation became impossible to hear. Disappointed, she moved back to her place at the table. She knew her family didn't like her much, but it hurt to hear them talk about her like that behind her back.

Meantime, everyone in the room turned toward the stage and stopped talking. The lights were dimmed and a statuesque, very curvaceous redhead moved up to the microphone and began to sing. Her sultry voice suited well the drawling, bluesy twenties music, and as Margo got carried away by the lovely, unfamiliar song, she forgot for a while that she wanted to cry and run away, and wondered where she had seen the singer before. The headlight followed the redhead as she sauntered across the makeshift stage, slowly and seductively, her sequined flapper-style evening dress shimmering under the powerful light. The young Frenchmen who sat with her and Jenny at the table followed her movements mesmerized, with eyes full of hunger and drooling mouths open, and for a second Margo regretted that she would never look like that. What it must feel, she wondered, to be so devastatingly beautiful and so incredibly talented.

Margo felt Jenny's hand pat hers understandingly, and she looked at her friend gratefully. They just had to accept that they had lost the attention of their boys forever.

When they excused themselves to go to the bathroom, the young men barely nodded. Margo looked over to where her family was sitting and she noticed that like every other man in the room, her cousin was staring at the singer. His gaze was hazy—possibly from too many whiskeys—and a small ball of saliva had settled in the corner of his mouth. Margo shuddered with disgust. She slipped away quickly before anyone at the aunts' table noticed that she was staring at them.

Chapter 7

Saffron Sigur

SAFFRON SIGUR, THE PRETTIEST WOMAN in the Yacht Club tonight, looked at herself in the bathroom mirror, and she liked what she saw. Her cat-like green eyes twinkled as she smiled to herself. A roomful of fools, she giggled, and one fool in particular. There were many obstacles to her plan, but they could be overcome. She had plenty of time. She would stay pretty for many more years, and God knew she was patient enough and willing to wait as long as it took. She adjusted her makeup, smoothed down her sequined dress, and turned around to leave, still smiling.

"Well look at what the cat dragged in," she said—not unkindly—to the woman entering the bathroom.

"Hello, Saffron. Nice to see you too," the newcomer grumbled.

"I see we look bitter as usual, Madeline."

"Of course I'm bitter. I have an idiot for a husband."

"I told you not to marry him. Remember that nice boy from high school? The one with the glasses and the freckles?"

"Who? Dave Berry?"

"Yes. I saw him the other day. He's the one you should have married. He was so in love with you."

"He had those horrible braces."

"Yes, but they eventually came off. And then he went to college and he became a Computer Engineer, and now he owns his own company. He makes money by the truckload."

"And you would know," Madeline said maliciously. "You always seem so well informed about the lives of the men around you."

"You don't have to say it like that. The point is, my friend that Robert didn't quite become everything that he could have, and now you're stuck with him and those horrible children."

"Yes, and his new hobby is to play all those Cole Porter songs. I wonder why." Madeline looked slyly at Saffron who quickly answered, "I had nothing to do with that. He's not my type."

Saffron looked at Madeline, frumpy, unglamorous, and unpleasant. They had been unlikely friends since childhood, and in spite of their physical differences and their frequent bickering, they understood each other well. Deep down, Saffron Sigur was fond of the unglamorous Madeline. She almost told her about something she had overheard the other day but changed her mind. She waited for her friend to leave the bathroom and looked after her pensively. Poor Madeline. What was the point of telling her? What she didn't know wouldn't hurt her. At least that's what they said.

On her way out, Saffron braced herself. She had to sing another set, but her heart wasn't in it. She wanted to be famous like her mom, Ava Sigur, but she didn't like Opera. This was her only other option—singing venues—but it was getting her nowhere.

Before she put her hand on the bathroom door, it opened forcefully and two young women barged in. Saffron looked at them and lifted an eyebrow in surprise.

"Hey, do I know you?" she asked Margo, bending down a couple of inches and looking at her closely.

"I don't think so," Margo sputtered shyly and took a small step back. "But we heard you sing and you were wonderful."

"Well, thank you kindly. I enjoy singing twenties Broadway music. Do you girls sing?" Jenny shook her head timidly but Margo answered right away.

"Sometimes. My cousin usually plays the piano after dinner at the aunts' house, and he found some Cole Porter sheet music in a garage sale the other day, so now he plays them on the piano part, and we both sing."

"Hmm. I'm sure you look familiar. Your cousin you said?"

"Yes, Robert Renaud. I'm staying with my aunts during the school holidays."

"Oh, I know who you are. You're Nicola Fontaine's daughter. I heard about her passing. You know, your mom and mine sang together many times, and people in the media followed their careers closely. Some thought they were great friends. I don't know how Nicola felt, but the truth is that my mom hated her. Sorry," Saffron blurted out and looked at the girls apologetically. "I shouldn't have said that, not like that. Your mother was an amazing artist. So you sing as well?"

"Only with my cousin after dinner," she answered, and the two girls looked at each other and laughed.

"Listen, Fontaine, I'm glad we met. We have to talk. There's something you ought to know. Let's have lunch tomorrow at the Parrot Joe Shack out by the Old Town. They make a killer fried catfish. Noon? Okay," Saffron added quickly. "I have to run. I have another set to sing."

Saffron hurried toward the musicians without looking back. She didn't owe the Fontaine kid anything, but she did feel obligated somehow. The poor thing looked so startled and innocent. How startled would she be if she knew what was going on behind her back? Saffron put her worries away and confidently stepped under the house light.

"Ladies and gentlemen, this next song…"

Chapter 8

Aunt Tilly's Not Feeling Well

"WHO WAS THAT WOMAN?" Jenny asked. "And how does she know you?"

"She's the daughter of a famous Opera singer. Her mom and mine had a legendary rivalry in spite of which they were amazing together. Concert halls were always sold out when they sang together. I don't remember meeting the daughter though, but she did look familiar."

The girls pushed their way through to their table. They passed close to the stage and looked up at the singer who smiled at them and gave them a little wave. A few couples were dancing slowly in a corner, oblivious to the outside world. They took a detour, carefully avoiding Aunt Beth and the rest of the family.

As they got closer, Margo noticed that Aunt Tilly didn't look her usual self. Her shoulders and her neck seemed to have stiffened, and her eyes were bulging, staring into some inner void. She was pale and still as a stone statue.

"Look, Jenny. I think my aunt is sick." She shoved her purse into Jenny's hand and started walking toward the family's table. Something was definitely off with her aunt. "Stay where you are. I don't want them to see you."

Margo pushed a couple of guests and a waiter aside and hurried to the table. She stooped down next to the old aunt, took her wrinkled face in her hands, and looked into her eyes. They were cloudy and unfocused. Her skin was hot and clammy. She got up and turned to the others who seemed very surprised to see her.

"Call an ambulance, Robert. Right now. Something's wrong with Aunt Tilly."

"Don't be dramatic, Margo. She's just drunk."

"No, she isn't drunk. She might have had a stroke. I've seen this before." She got back down and tried again to make eye contact, but her aunt remained confused and unresponsive. "What are you waiting for, Robert? For her to die?" Margo got up brusquely and yelled at her cousin. "Call an ambulance now, Robert, before it's too late."

When she realized that Robert wasn't going to do anything to get help, Margo called out as loud as she could if there was a doctor in the house. There was a commotion among the guests, and the music stopped, and people stared curiously in her direction. Pretty soon several doctors stepped up to Aunt Tilly and examined her eyes and her pulse. One of them called an ambulance while another one kept the other guests away from Aunt Tilly to give her breathing space.

Margo was shaking with fear, holding the old aunt's limp hand, cold as dead already, counting the seconds for help to arrive, terrified that it wouldn't get there on time and her dear aunt would die. But it was a short distance to St. Hildegard's and within two or three minutes, she heard the sirens of the ambulance bleating into the distance. She breathed with relief when she saw two paramedics jog into the room with a stretcher and with an oxygen mask that they placed on Tilly's face. After a quick consensus, one of the doctors nodded and followed them out of the dance hall, and before Margo could blink twice, they were all gone.

For the most part, the Ball was over. People milled about curiously, but after the ambulance left with Aunt Tilly, there was nothing left to see, and everyone went back to their business. Suddenly, Margo and Jenny were left alone in a room full of upset chairs, spilled drinks, and remnants of food on the floor. Guests were exiting through the large French doors that led to the back of the Yacht Club and the golf course.

Margo grabbed Jenny's hand and pulled her to the exit. There was nothing they could do but go back home. They were on their way to pick up their coats and their backpacks at the entrance when the singer rushed past them. She stopped for a second and looked at Margo very seriously.

"Fontaine, we've really got to talk. Tomorrow at the Parrot Joe Shack at noon. Be there." And with that, she vanished into the crowd.

The evening ruined, Margo and Jenny sat down on a bench by the waterfront and took their high-heeled shoes off. Nobody was in a mood to change clothes, but the shoes had to come off. Margo massaged her aching feet. The house on East Albatross was suddenly a long, long way away.

The orchestra was playing again. Maybe the Club was trying to salvage the evening in spite of the "food poisoning" rumors that were circulating already.

Out on the water, fancy little sailboats bobbed on the shimmering water under the light of the fragile moon, their strings of multicolored lights brightening the midnight sky and reflecting on the water, their flags and sails billowing in the warm summer breeze. The girls sat for a while, watching the night, waiting for the last of the champagne to dissipate from their bodies.

"What a sad way to end the day," Jenny said. "I hope your aunt will be okay."

"I hope so too, but she's so old and fragile."

"What do you think happened to her?"

"I don't know. I saw something like that once in a science show on TV. It was a program about strokes, and it looked just like what happened to my aunt."

"Is that curable?"

"Yes, I think so. But only if the patient gets to the hospital on time."

"The ambulance came very fast."

"Yes. And there were several doctors. Maybe she'll make it." Her voice sounded convinced, as if she really believed what she had just said, but deep down, it began to dawn on her that too many things were going wrong all of a sudden, and her aunt might not survive after all.

Chapter 9

Meet Mimi

ALL BUILT OF WOODEN LOGS, the Parrot Joe Shack was famously old, almost older than the rest of the town. Sitting right at the water's edge, with a sweeping view of the bay and of any approaching marauder ship, rumor had it that pirates had first built the shack as a place to get together and enjoy a pint of beer from time to time, from where they could keep their eyes on their ships and crews. They had a tacit rule that they would never draw swords against each other while in Half Moon Bay, and according to history, they never did. Eventually, a number of aging pirates and their women settled in the pretty bay and lived there happily ever after until their houses were ravaged in a series of hurricanes in the late eighteen hundreds. Only the Parrot Joe Shack remained always standing, seemingly immune to bad weather. And because of that, the town adopted it as their most historic building and kept a watchful eye on it with views to preserve it for posterity.

Margo stepped into the diner and looked around for the unmistakable red hair. The singer from the Yacht Club hadn't arrived yet. The Parrot Joe Shack was surprisingly busy with lunchtime customers, and she pushed her way around the jostling group by the counter waiting to be served, to get to the back of the spacious hall where a large fan moved the hot air lazily back and forth, and there seemed to be more space to breathe.

A young waitress with frizzy hair and a rolled-up red bandanna around her neck swooshed by and stopped in front of her. Her name tag read Rosalie. Rosalie said hello and grinned. "If you follow me now, Miss, there's a couple about to leave in the corner and you can take their table before the crowd notices." Margo grinned back and followed her.

She sat down gratefully and ordered an iced tea and a catfish burger. She loved the smell of fried seafood, and she especially loved fried catfish. She looked around curiously. The nautical interior included tables made of salvaged boat wood, stuffed fish mounted on worm-eaten plaques, and an oversized fish tank by the checkout counter. The ceiling was decorated with nets, buoys, and boating equipment. It looked very much the way it probably had way back when the shack was first built.

Halfway through her iced tea, she spotted the singer's cascade of red curly hair coming in through the entrance. Margo waived furiously from the back of the room. The woman cast furtive glances about the restaurant until she spotted her.

She sat down and introduced herself.

"Hello again, Fontaine. My name is Saffron Sigur."

"Oh, yes. Hello, you're Ava Sigur's daughter. You don't look like your mother at all."

"I know. I take after my dad."

"I remember when she sang with my mom a few years back, right here in Half Moon Bay. She held an unlit cigarette with a very long filter in her hand. She told me that singing duets with my mom always made her want to take up smoking again."

"Yup, that's her. Listen, you must be wondering why I asked you to lunch." She turned toward the young waitress and said, "Rosalie, bring me a crawfish salad and an iced tea." Then she continued talking to Margo.

"If I told you out of the blue that I'm here to warn you that your life's in danger, you'd think I'm crazy and you would ignore my warning. So let me tell you a little about myself and what it is that I do."

Margo just blinked and nodded in a daze. Finally, she managed to say okay.

"I'm the Society Pages Editor for the Half Moon Gazette, which is a glorified gossip page. I do a lot of research for work, and of course, we specialize in the rich and famous. You know the type of article: what she wore to this concert, where he spent his weekend and with whom, who showed up at the Krewe Queen's Gala, that sort of thing. All very harmless. And then we make sure that we take pictures that make them look glamorous, to keep them happy."

"I didn't know there were any rich and famous people in Half Moon Bay."

"You'd be surprised, my dear. There's a lot of old money among the original Southern families around here. And they'll do anything to preserve their status and their heritage, and I mean anything.

"But occasionally, I come across information that could destroy a career or cause tremendous and irreparable harm. I admit that I've been tempted to publish some of those stories because, well, because powerful people have little regard for the rest of us. But I want you to know that I never have. I'm not the type of reporter who would sell her soul for a few extra papers in circulation."

Margo looked at Saffron waiting for an explanation to this very long prelude and nodded, but all Saffron seemed to want to do was to play with her salad. She moved a tiny crawfish back and forth on her plate and finally popped it in her mouth.

"So, what are you trying to say that you're not saying?" she asked, getting impatient. "Does this have anything to do with my family?"

"Well, maybe." It was obvious that Saffron was very uncomfortable. "I should have planned better on how to tell you all this. I have no proof, but it might have something to do with them."

"Just tell me already. You make me feel like running away." Indeed, Margo was about to jump up from her chair and bolt. Too many things were going wrong in her life. This was fast becoming the last straw.

"Okay, then. So someone's trying to kill you. My first thought was your family. There's a lot you probably don't know about them. You've been gone forever and you really don't know anything about them. Your family is pretty rich, and from what I've heard, pretty ruthless. They have houses and investments, and your cousin Robert has never worked a serious job in his life, yet he lives a life of leisure. Maybe he felt that his financial security was being threatened."

Margo was horrified. "That's a terrible thing to say. Robert would never try to hurt me..." And then she suddenly remembered the familiar handwriting on the to-do list on the sheet of paper that fell out of the sheet music. She had never paid attention to Robert's handwriting, but could it be his? Could he have written all those nasty letters that had tormented her down the years? She shook her head. She couldn't believe it. She refused to believe it. But the doubt remained.

"Now Margo, I didn't say he would be capable of hurting you, I just said that that was my first thought. The thing is that there have been many scandals in your family, and there's that will thing that nobody ever talks about. But thanks to the money they spread around, they have been able to keep all these things quiet."

"What will?"

"Exactly. That's what I asked myself."

"I'm not sure I like where this is going." Margo sat up straight in her chair and put the burger down.

"Yes, sorry. I'm distressing you, and I didn't mean to do that."

Saffron put a lovely manicured hand on Margo's shaking arm, soothing her. "This might not make any sense to you, but I'm really trying to help you. Listen. Because it is my job to write about people, I've developed the habit of watching them. Snooping on them, you know? When something unusual happens, I pay attention, and I follow up.

"But let me start at the beginning. Madeline—your cousin's wife—and I grew up together. We've always been friends. We went to the same schools and frequented the same circles. Anyway, I know she's not the nicest person in the world, but I'm kind of sorry for her, for having married that idiot that's giving her such a miserable life."

"My cousin Robert."

"Yes. So there are some new people in town, mostly smooth looking men. They are spending a lot of money, playing golf, hanging out in the Yacht Club asking too many questions. Last week, Madeline went to a Church thing with some friends, and afterward, they were sitting at a table at *Frederique's* close to some of those pretentious rich dudes and she overheard a very strange conversation. All the men except two got up and left the table. Her back was to them, and so she couldn't see who was who, nor did she recognize their voices.

"So these two guys started talking about a hit. You know, like when you hire someone to kill someone."

"Yes, go on."

"When Madeline heard that, she started paying attention, just out of curiosity. Imagine her surprise and her shock when she realized that they were talking about you. Some woman called Kathy Mason had hired someone to kill you."

Margo's eyes got big as saucers. This was beginning to sound like a bad joke. She briefly considered getting up and leaving because she really didn't want to hear any more. This was all nonsense. But she did want to. She had to find out. "No way."

"I know. Hard to believe. But they mentioned you by name, and Madeline got very worried. They talked about that for a few minutes and then Madeline gathered her courage—because she was terrified—and she turned around to get a look at them. Unfortunately at that minute the other guys came back and they all got up from their chairs, and Madeline didn't know any of them anyway, so that was that."

"To kill me? But why on earth?"

"Well, that was why I first thought about the will. But hold on. Let me finish. So she was telling me all this at lunch the other day, and I decided to look into it. You might not realize it but Madeline likes you more than she admits. She's not very demonstrative and comes across as sort of snooty and cold, but she has a heart like the rest of us."

"I think you're wrong there. I heard her talking about me behind my back at the Regatta party, and what she said wasn't pretty. It was mean and cruel."

"I'm not here to analyze Madeline. She might have been in a petty mood. She gets like that sometimes. The point is that she asked me to look into what she heard because she was worried, so I tried to find out more about the guys. I checked with my sources, I asked around. These guys they're all ruthless, rich, and arrogant. You know the type. They arrive on their yachts, they spread their money around and try to hook up with the local girls. But none of them seemed to fit the bill of a killer for hire. Then I tried to find out who this Kathy

Mason was. There are hundreds of women called Kathy Mason and none of them live in Half Moon Bay.

"Could it be a pretend name?"

"Yes, of course. It very well might be. Anyway, so I hit a wall and then got busy with other stuff and quit looking. Truth is that I forgot about it. But then came the Yacht Club party. I was walking just a few steps behind you and your friend last night, and I saw how you almost got run over. I could tell it was no accident. That driver was determined to run you over, even if he had to run the whole town over to get to you. Of course, I didn't know who you were then, but I was angry at the stupid driver like everyone else was. I tried to catch his license plate number, but it all happened too fast.

"And then I ran into you in the bathroom and found out who you were. At that moment everything clicked. I remembered what Madeline told me about the hit on you, and I felt that I had to warn you."

"I still don't know why anyone would want to kill me. I haven't made any enemies, I don't think."

"You're rich and you have all those skeletons in your closet."

"No, I don't."

"Oh, honey, you have more skeletons in your closet than anyone else I know."

"Like what?" Margo asked, looking suspiciously at Saffron.

"Well, for starters, there's the vanishing will. Then, there's that story of the dead body. Nobody has actually seen it, but rumors were floating around back when. And then, there's Mimi and your grandfather François. Oh, look at that, and here she comes. I'll be darned. I'll have to tell you some other time. Hello Mimi," Saffron called the newcomer and waved her hands. "Come meet Nicola Fontaine's daughter."

Margo looked at the woman approaching the table and resented the intrusion. They had met before, not formally, but just to nod and say hi. Mimi was the owner of the Pirate Bay Hotel. Mimi had always been nice to her, but after what Saffron said, she now looked at the woman with different eyes. How could this woman have something to do with Grand-père François and her family skeletons?

Mimi squeezed past the customers and approached their table. She was middle-aged and slightly overweight. Her long, tightly curled hair was picked up on top of her head in a loose bun that flattered her heart-shaped face. Her skin was dark as if she had had an African ancestor. Despite being middle-aged, her demeanor remained that of a coquettish young woman, and Margo admitted that she must have been beautiful in her youth because there was plenty of charm left in her. Her skin was still smooth, and her hair had very few strands of white.

With a quick "Better go", Saffron jumped up and headed for the door. Margo stared at her back, wondering what all had just happened.

"Beware the bringer of gossip," Mimi told her and sat down uninvited.

"Beg pardon?"

"What has she been telling you, that woman?"

"Umm, nothing much. Just talking about last night's party."

"I heard you almost got yourself run over," Mimi said lifting an eyebrow. Margo blinked fast, wondering if an answer was expected. "You need to be careful. There's always evil lurking in the bushes. Half Moon Bay might not be the best place for you, you know." Mimi got up with a soft grunt and smiled at Margo. "Well, I just wanted to come say hi. Was nice seeing you again. You take care of yourself, now."

Mimi walked away as unexpectedly as she had appeared, brushing in between customers and vanishing from her view. Margo looked at her catfish burger and at Saffron's uneaten salad and realized that she wasn't hungry anymore. She threw a twenty on the table and got up without noticing that two tables over, a group of young hard-looking men stared at her as she went by, and one of them asked, "Is she the one?" and another one answered, "I think so." He took a Polaroid photograph out of his pocket and looked at it closely. "Yes," he repeated. "I think so."

Chapter 10

At The Hospital

THE SAINT HILDEGARD MEMORIAL HOSPITAL of Half Moon Bay stood cheerfully behind St. Quintian's Church in all its colonial glory. It had once been—when young women still flocked to take vows—a teaching convent, with enormous schoolrooms and spacious bedrooms for the mostly indigent young pupils who were lucky enough to get into the school.

While many convents were famous for the extreme discipline imparted by the nun teachers, Saint Hildegard's differed in that most of the young novices and nuns had been known for their kindness and their easygoing attitudes. Perhaps it was the serenity of the scenery or the sweetness of the oranges and figs that grew everywhere. Or perhaps it was simply that living by the sea filled the little nuns' hearts with so much joy that it didn't ever allow them to get angry.

In any case, when the last of the nuns grew old and died, and Saint Hildegard's was converted from convent into hospital, there was so much goodwill in the air, so many good vibes, so many good memories, that patients seemed to heal almost miraculously in a very short amount of time. There were even efforts to request a renewed Sainthood for St. Hildegard—if there could be such a thing—because she was so very much loved.

Like everyone in Half Moon Bay who had ever had to go to the hospital, Margo mounted the steps with enthusiasm and the confidence that Aunt Tilly would get well soon—as everyone always did—almost by a miracle. So it was a shock when she saw the old aunt surrounded by tubes, and vein drips, and all kinds of beeping machines.

Aunt Tilly was wearing an oxygen mask that helped her breathe. She took in the air laboriously, and her lungs made a whistling, rushing sound. Margo hurried to her side, horrified, her heart hopping in her chest like a trapped bird. She sat quietly by the bedside and held Aunt Tilly's fragile, shriveled hand. After a while, the old lady opened her eyes and smiled. Her skin was sallow, almost green, and her eyes had a milky haze that had a hard time focusing. But she was lucid.

She tried to say something but the mask made her words unintelligible, so she carefully lifted a hand and removed it.

"Don't do that, Aunt Tilly. You won't be able to breathe."

"It's okay, my dear. Just for a minute or two. How are you?"

"I'm all right, Aunt Tilly. How are you? You collapsed at the party, and I thought you had a stroke."

"That's what Beth and Robert thought, but it's not what happened. Someone tried to poison me. I know it."

"But what did the doctor say?"

"He said I didn't have a stroke."

"So what does he think really happened?"

Aunt Tilly hesitated. Margo kept waiting for her to answer, but she just stared at the walls behind her. Her breathing was getting raspier.

"Aunt Tilly, you have to put your oxygen mask back on. You're not breathing properly."

The old woman suddenly grabbed Margo's arm with an unexpected strength and looked at her. There seemed to be a lot of fear in those milky, hazy eyes.

"Listen to me, child. Listen to me carefully. Don't tell anyone, but the doctor agrees with me that I've been poisoned."

"Oh, but Aunt Tilly, how's that even possible? Why would anyone want to poison you? He must be mistaken."

"Don't scoff, dear. The doctor's running some tests, and then we'll know for sure. But the important thing is that he believes me, and he agrees with me. Sweet doctor, he's a longtime friend."

"But poisoned? Who would want to poison you?"

"I can think of a few people, you know." Aunt Tilly was having a harder and harder time talking and was gasping for air.

"Please put your oxygen mask back on. I can tell you're having a hard time breathing."

"I will, but listen," she whispered. Her bony hand, crisscrossed with swollen greenish veins grabbed Margo's ever so gently. "Listen, child, I have to warn you. You're in danger. Get out of the house. Go back to school and don't come back. Ever."

"But I always come back to be with you."

"I won't be here. If I've been poisoned, it's only a matter of time before they come back and put an end to me."

"Please don't talk like that," Margo said, trying to quell the panic in her voice.

"Do as I say, child. Go away as far as you can, because they have long arms and they will never leave you alone until they've sucked all the life out of you."

"Who, Aunt Tilly? Who?" Margo realized that she was shaking her aunt's arm, and one of the tubes came out of her arm, and the machine behind her started beeping loudly. In a matter of seconds, nurses were at the foot of the bed, ushering her out of the room, getting ready to administer the appropriate care.

Margo turned back to her aunt, trying to at least tell her she was sorry, but one of the nurses grabbed her arm and pulled her out of the room. Before she left, she turned toward her aunt and looked at her, hoping to catch her eyes. But they were blank again, looking at nothing in particular. She was oblivious to whatever had just happened: the beeping of the machines, the running of the nurses, the sudden way Margo had to leave. She begged and she cried to be allowed to stay, to say goodbye to Aunt Tilly at least, but in a matter of seconds, she was standing in the corridor in front of her aunt's room, and the door was being firmly shut, right in front of her face.

Chapter 11

Rosa Nesta's Chicken

THE FAINT SOUND of Rosa Nesta's radio music filtered out from behind the kitchen. Aunt Beth was out, running errands somewhere. Robert—grim-faced as usual—had shown up earlier to get her.

The old house moaned and groaned under the threat of the incoming storm. Outside, the wind had picked up and was beating the branches of the centenarian oak trees against the dusty window screens, like the fingers of night creatures, scratching against the windows, begging to be let inside.

Without Aunt Beth's shrill voice constantly complaining, and without the never-ending clop-clop of her walking stick echoing through the unlit corridors, the place suddenly felt as gloomy as a mausoleum, cloying with the smell of mildew and decay. Lightning struck with violence and made the lamplights flicker, and Margo sighed with worry. Not the electricity, please not the electricity, she whispered.

Up in the attic, the cats were restless, scared of the storm. Ice, the big white one, balancing himself precariously on the narrow window sill, stared with big startled eyed into the darkness outside—terrified but unable to look away—and Fenway, the little calico, wouldn't stop crying, begging him to come down.

"I'm hungry," Jenny said with the nonchalance of someone used to tropical storms.

"I know. Me too. Let's go downstairs."

"Is Aunt Beth back?"

"No, I don't think so. We would have heard her. Smells like Mrs. Cook made chicken again. Let's go find out."

On hearing the word *chicken*, Ice jumped down from the ledge and Fenway stopped crying. They ran to the door and looked expectantly at the girls. Margo smiled and opened the attic door.

The storm was moving in steadily from the sea. Thunder shook the world with a rhythmic persistence coming ever closer to Half Moon Bay. Yet here in the secluded hallway, you could barely hear the wind beating on the house. But a sudden lightning flash illuminated the stairwell and Ice's impossibly white, shiny fur lit up like ice crystals. Little Fenway, terrified of everything, shrieked and started shaking, and Jenny picked her up so she wouldn't cry. Then they tiptoed down the creaking stairs.

Mrs. Cook had magically whipped up something tropical that sent fingers of aromas all over the house. As a rule of thumb, Mrs. Cook's chicken dishes drove the cats insane, and they usually scratched big patches of paint off the attic door leaving long stretches of narrow claw marks, begging to be allowed out, until Margo finally relented. So it was that very quietly they opened the door to the kitchen and found themselves face to face with Snail—the butler—and Mrs. Cook.

"It's okay, girls. Come in, come in," said Rosa Nesta, wiping her hands on her *Kiss The Cook* apron. "It's just us. Dinner's ready. And you better eat fast, all four of you, because Miss Beth will be back any minute." She turned back to her wooden board and started chopping some baked chicken for the cats.

"Is Miss Tilly doing any better?" asked Snail. He put the Brasso and the dirty cloth on the kitchen table and looked up sadly at Margo and her friend. "You know, young Margo, that we are very fond of Miss Tilly."

"Yes, Mr. Snail, I know. She isn't doing so well. I'm afraid for her. But the doctors at St. Hildegard's are good, right? They will cure her." Snail and the cook looked at each other, and a secret signal seemed to pass between them because then they both turned to Margo and said way too enthusiastically, of course, they will.

"Someone tried to run us over at the party yesterday," Jenny said, her mouth full of *Paella*. "This jeep came out of nowhere, sent people scattering in its path, ran over some stalls on the Boardwalk, and came right at us. And I could swear that they were aiming right at us, but

Margo says who would want to kill us? So she thinks it must have been an accident."

"I said that yesterday," Margo objected, fork in hand, "but I'm not saying that anymore. I got two warnings today, so maybe I should take this more seriously."

"Maybe you should, young Margo. I'm about to give you your third warning," Snail said.

"Yes. You might as well be careful," added the cook, shaking her head vigorously. "Something is going on that I don't like. Evil stalks this house." At that, Margo almost burst out laughing but quickly stopped. Rosa Nesta was absolutely serious. She gesticulated wildly with that big kitchen knife in her hand, as a woman possessed. Her eyes were wide and troubled, and Margo noticed that her mouth was moving silently as if she was casting protection spells against evil. Snail's eyes looked down quietly and he continued polishing the silver. An ominous silence fell over the little group. Then, they heard the front door creaking open, and a set of jingling keys being thrown in the glass bowl on the table by the entrance, and Margo, Jenny, and her two clever cats, all ran upstairs as fast and quiet as the wind, while the clop-clop of Aunt Beth's walking stick got ever closer.

Chapter 12

Marie Duval

DARKNESS FELL ON HALF MOON BAY as another magnificent sunset said good night to the land. In the hospital, silence fell. TV's were turned off, and one by one the patients dropped off to sleep. The nurses came and went busily, settling everyone in for the night, their kind and tired faces reflected in the windows of the rooms where they worked.

Marie Duval, wishing she was anywhere else but at St. Hildegard's, watched the last nurse of the third floor say good night and close the hallway door behind her and contemplated the long, lonely night ahead. Just for tonight, just as a favor to another nurse, she was doing night duty on the Intensive Care floor. But she didn't like the third floor. Nurses said that it was haunted. A number of them had sworn that they had seen St. Hildegard herself walking the corridors of the former convent, arm in arm with a pregnant nun who legend said had thrown herself out of this same third floor after her baby was stillborn.

Of course, Marie knew that this was not possible. St. Hildegard had been long dead on another continent when the convent was first built. But some of her writings and an old medieval portrait had place of reverence in the library. Nonsense, she told herself. Objects can't be haunted. It was the long, dark nights, and the creaking floorboards and the wind whistling in through the windows that made people imagine that there were ghosts in the place.

Unaccustomed to the quiet, Marie Duval looked around suspiciously. In every dark corner, she thought she saw lurking a stealthy shadow. Every smallest noise had to be an intruder. She told herself there was nothing to be scared of and picked up her book with determination, but her mind was on the disturbing silence, so she kept reading the same paragraph over and over again, unable to take her mind off her fear.

The church clock rang eleven times and she looked up, startled. The book had fallen out of her hands and it was lying on the floor, closed. She picked it up, embarrassed at having dozed off. Beyond the chimes, she was pretty sure she had heard something, a rustling, like a stiff fabric brushing against wallpaper. She sat very still with eyes wide with fear, listening intently. Nothing. It was nothing. It was just her imagination.

Marie got up from her chair, trying to walk without shaking. She turned on the big overhead light, and the whole floor came to life. That's what she should have done, to begin with. The brightness woke her up and gave her a kick of courage. There, she told herself. There's nothing to fear. She patted her hair and smoothed down her nurse's uniform. She might as well check on her patients while she was up.

You can tell me whatever you want, she muttered to herself as she walked around, but dark and quiet hospitals are scary at night. Too many corners, too many shadows. The big light stays on the rest of the night, and that's all there is to it. She nodded to herself, and she went from room to room, opening doors carefully and making sure that all the patients of Intensive Care were sleeping with their IV's and machines properly connected. Then, she went back to the desk and sat down, and now wide awake and somewhat braver, she picked up her book again and began to read.

Right about midnight, when she was beginning to worry she might doze off again, Marie Duval thought she smelled something funny in the air. It wasn't a nasty smell, but floral, pleasant, like lilacs, and she turned around surprised, trying to figure out where it was coming from. After a few seconds, the scent of lilacs dissipated, and she lost interest, so she went back to her book.

It was turning into one of those unusual nights, she told herself as she turned a page of the book. First, those sounds out by the staircase, and now this smell. Well, the morning couldn't come fast enough. And she was never volunteering for night shift ever again. She was too much of a coward to go through this again.

The smell came back with a vengeance a few minutes later, and she inhaled the familiar scent happily, and she felt giddy, as if she had had too much wine, or had gotten up too suddenly from a chair. She should investigate where it was coming from, but all of a sudden she was very tired and uninterested. Should she close her eyes—just for a few minutes—and take a quick nap? Nobody had to find out, right? All the patients were on the mend, and all connected to machines that would beep if something went wrong.

The urge to close her eyes got stronger and stronger. Soon, Marie Duval stopped fighting it. She looked around one last time to make sure that everything was well and thought she saw a shadow slink through the corridor from the stairs. But she was beyond caring. She put her head down on the crook of her arm and within seconds was fast asleep. She never saw the shadow walk past her, nor did she see it enter one of the rooms and close the door behind it. To Marie Duval, nothing mattered anymore.

Chapter 13

Recital

IF YOU WERE very, very careful when you climbed out of the attic window, you could crawl onto a narrow ledge on the roof where you could—if you were young and fearless—sit and enjoy the spectacular view that encompassed most of the bay. It made you feel as if you were sitting on the top of the world. Ice and Fenway, happy to get some freedom and fresh air scampered all around the roof, surefooted, sniffing and investigating everything. It was a moment of absolute perfection. The sky was clear blue, not a cloud in sight. The day hadn't become too hot or too humid yet, and birds of all shapes and sizes twittered in the tree branches enjoying the lovely weather.

The Regatta was still over a week away, and yet the sleepy town had already been invaded by tourists in straw hats and multicolored Hawaiian shirts who continued to arrive in swarms like locusts, and it seemed that the little seaside town would soon be unable to accommodate another living soul. Margo wondered where all those people were planning to sleep since the only hotel in town was already full.

She watched the neighbor from across the street bring out his trash followed by his big yellow dog, and the dog sensed either them or the cats because it looked in their direction and barked, and the neighbor looked up as well and waved the girls hello. He was a friendly older man with luxurious white hair, still quite handsome. Margo had the feeling that he was in love with Rosa Nesta, the cook.

He always made an effort to run into her when she was heading to the grocery store, or to church. This had been going on for years, and yet Rosa Nesta either didn't notice or didn't care because nothing ever seemed to come of it.

Margo was happy to be with Jenny, her dearest friend. Summers and Christmases at the aunts' were so lonely, so bleak. She sometimes went to the beach or sang in the church choir when extra singers were needed, but that was it, and by the end of her stay, she was always more than ready to get back to school, and to her friends.

"Should we even consider going to the recital tonight, with your aunt so sick and all?" Jenny asked. She was petting little Fenway who was sitting in her lap, purring.

"The doctor said Aunt Tilly is getting better by the day and will make a full recovery. Since she will be coming back home soon, I don't feel guilty about going out. Now, if she was getting worse, I wouldn't even dream of it."

"Why do you want to go so badly anyway?"

"An old nemesis of my mom's is singing with Ava Sigur, Saffron's mom in the Opera House." Margo took one look at Jenny's disappointed face, and she laughed. "Oh, Jenny, I know you don't like Opera music that much. Why don't you stay home and hang out with the cats, or get started on those school papers while I go and check things out?"

"I guess I could make a sacrifice and miss the Opera. What is a nemesis?" Jenny asked with an eyebrow up.

"You know, rival."

"They have those in the Opera world?" Jenny asked surprised.

Margo laughed again. "You wouldn't believe the kind of drama and backstabbing that goes on in the world of music. Not to mention mishaps, misunderstanding, and feuds."

"Seriously?"

Margo giggled. "You probably haven't heard any Opera Singer and light bulb jokes then."

"Well, no."

"Let me ask you. How many sopranos does it take to screw in a light bulb? Two. One to get up on the chair and screw it in, and the other one to kick the chair out from under her."

"Oh, no. That bad?"

"Oh, yes. In the early 1700s, the Italian sopranos Faustina Bordoni and Francesca Cuzzoni started beating up on each other on stage, during the performance. They tore each other's wigs and clothes off and finally had to be dragged off stage, semi-naked, to the delighted hoots and the whistles of the audience.

"Rivalries run deep when places in the limelight are so few and so competitive. Even Antonio Salieri confessed at some point to murdering Amadeus Mozart because it drove him nuts that Mozart was so famous and he was only second best."

"But that doesn't happen much anymore, does it?"

Margo laughed. "You mustn't have heard about the time that Pavarotti and Renata Scotto refused to hold hands and look at each other while singing a love song. They insisted on standing on separate sides of the stage, angrily, making no eye contact, while the theater manager beat her head against the wall in despair."

"Why were they fighting?"

"It seemed like such a small thing. During a San Francisco production of *La Gioconda*, Pavarotti took a final, unscheduled solo bow—you know, all by himself—while Scotto stood by furiously. She stormed off the stage and uttered an Italian obscenity, really loudly, which was unfortunately recorded on television. Later on in life, she lamented that she had lost such a good friend, but never referred to him by name again. Not once. Instead, Scotto always referred to Pavarotti as "a certain tenor".

"And this nemesis of your mom's is singing tonight?"

"Yes. Her name is Katherine de Messian. She showed up one day out of nowhere a couple of years before my mom's death, completely taking the musical world by surprise. I guess my mom felt threatened. She had worked hard to become famous and here was this upstart without any stage experience taking some of her best roles away, and from that moment on, she became her mortal enemy. Opera people are very passionate people."

"So who is she, this Katherine de something?"

"All I can tell you is that she's very good and very famous, but nobody knows anything about her. She has no past. I've looked, I've checked, and there's nothing online anywhere about her. Obviously, Katherine de Messian is just her stage name. I've heard her a couple of times and she's amazing. Anyway. The thing is that there is so little around me that was part of my mom's life that I feel that I owe it to her to go see her enemies sing. I don't know if that makes any sense to you."

Margo and Jenny watched the swimmers in the bay. A sudden cool wind swept through and picked up the flags on the sailboats and the Boardwalk, and made them flap stiffly. A couple of the swimmers had ventured farther out than it was prudent, and Margo wondered at their recklessness. Didn't they remember this wasn't called Shark Bayou for nothing?

Margo passed the binoculars to Jenny and let her gaze follow the sandy beach to where two lifeguards sat in their tower wearing their red and yellow t-shirts. They looked like miniature figures in a toy town set. Then she heard wild whistling and saw one of the lifeguards running on the sand, waving his arms.

"What's going on, Jenny?" she asked.

"I think it's okay. The swimmers are turning around. They swam too far out."

"The fools," Margo said. She put her hand in front of her eyes and squinted against the slanting sun in direction of the Yacht Club. An enormous yacht had just anchored, and a smaller boat was heading in its direction to pick up the travelers. She wondered at all the sudden activity in the sleepy little town. How much did a yacht like that cost anyway? And how did a relatively low-key regatta attract so many rich people? And why?"

Walking gingerly to not ruin her elegant high-heel shoes, Margo crossed Salt Water Drive, looking carefully both ways before she stepped off the curb. She stopped at the Sky Harbor Boulevard and with a sinking feeling realized that she was afraid to cross the busy street. She wiped her sweaty palms on her dress. She still had the bruises from falling down when she and Jenny were almost run over. And all those warnings were getting to her. So she screened the street in one direction and then the other, looking for the jeep that had tried to kill her, and when the walking light turned green, she crossed with other people, staying close to them, trying not to listen to the hammering of her heart.

Alive on the other side of the boulevard despite her fears, she started walking toward Independence Park from where the front doors of St. Quintian's Church, the Town Hall, and the newly renovated colonial Opera House faced each other.

The original Half Moon Bay French Theater had hosted its first Opera sometime during the Christmas season of 1850 with the gala performance of Rossini's *Guillaume Tell*. It had been love at first sight. The locals fell not only for the music but for the pageantry of the Opera scene. Old European families who missed their more glamorous lives at Court, rejoiced at having the chance to live for a few hours at least, the way they had back home.

Agnes Makóczy

By the 1860s, any Opera or Ballet Ensemble visiting New Orleans—already an important city with a very active cultural life—was being invited to perform in Half Moon Bay. There was always plenty of money to pay for the best. The most famous Opera singers, the most accomplished Ballet troupes enchanted the audiences of the French Theater. The gifted young soprano Adelina Patti sang there, at barely 17 years old, just prior to her debut on the international scene, appearing in Donizetti's *Lucia di Lammermoor* and then, during the remainder of the season, in *Il Trovatore*, *Rigoletto*, and other operas that were popular at the time. The reputation of the French Theater grew.

During WWI, under the threat of submarine warfare, inviting European operatic ensembles was impossible, so the town shuttered the exquisitely carved wood and beaten copper doors of their lovely theater house and waited for peace. But bad luck struck in September of 1918. During the early morning hours, the old theater caught fire and by the next morning at dawn, it lay in smoldering ruins. It took 20 years to rebuild, now more spacious and more luxurious than ever. Since then, and with better acoustics, the French Theater was now renamed the Pierre-Alexandre Monsigny or just the *Monsigny* for short.

A well-dressed crowd was gathered at the foot of the marble sphinx that graced the entrance to the beautiful Monsigny. It was the local tradition to wear all your jewelry for such events because you had to try to outdo each other in riches. And of course, Saffron Sigur was there with her crew from the Half Moon Gazette, taking notes and photographs for her Society Pages while children and other park visitors gawked.

She had almost reached the steps to the Monsigny when an unusual sight made her turn her head. It was a barely perceived movement from the corner of her eyes, but one that made her look twice. An enormous fawn-colored dog had shrugged itself out from behind a clump of azalea bushes, barking like it was a life-and-death situation, and galloped across the park in a straight line toward the spot where Margo was standing—surprised—trying to figure out why that bark sounded so familiar. Like in a moment of *déjà-vu*, she was transported to the distant past and remembered that forgotten dog, the one that had saved her life. What was his name? Paco! But how could this be Paco, after all those years?

Then, all of a sudden, the dog lunged at Margo—in what football players call a tackle—and caught her on the chest with two huge paws, making her lose her balance and stumble. The dog was whimpering and barking, all at the same time. Margo tried to disentangle herself, to catch her breath, but the dog was just too excited to see her. Hopping on his hind legs, he wagged his tail wildly, licking her neck and her face with a big blubbery tongue. There was no doubt that he had recognized her, and from all the blubber, there was no doubt that this was Paco.

Margo got down on her knees and hugged the dog and started to cry without any reason. Sweet old Paco, what was he doing here? Unless Jack had abandoned his beloved old puppy, he had to be somewhere near. With tears streaming down her face, she scanned the crowd for Jack but couldn't see him. All of a sudden, her past came rushing back like a train out of control. She remembered her mom and the ache of the emptiness that her death had left behind, and that made her cry harder. Oh, Paco. He sat patiently with his tongue lolling while Margo kneeled in her pretty evening gown and held him. She cherished the familiar smell of his sweaty fur. He drooled over her arm and her clothes and didn't move a muscle while Margo held him and talked to him. And then, just as suddenly—as if he had heard his name being called—Paco detached himself from

Margo's arms and ran away, his ears lopping as he went. He never looked back, but he kept wagging his tail until he vanished into the night.

Someone came over to Margo, helped her up, and asked her if she was okay. She said yes, thank you, wiped her tears, and looked around wistfully. If she had hoped for just one second that Jack would appear looking for his dog, she was disappointed. The dog was now long gone, and there was no Jack to be seen.

She walked up the steps to the Opera House knowing that now she looked like a dishrag, but there was no time to go home and change. She picked up her ticket at the entrance and avoided the gaze of the elegant patrons who whispered about her appearance behind her back.

The musicians in the orchestra pit were tuning their instruments, and Margo hurried to find her seat, trying not to step on any toes or evening gowns as she squeezed herself into her seat. Curtain call couldn't come soon enough, and within minutes the lights were turned off, and she had a chance to regain her composure in the darkened hall.

Katherine de Messian was as formidable as she remembered her. Big-chested, with an enormous amount of long blond hair, she would have made a good Viking wife. And she definitely owned the stage. Her presence was so overwhelming that she eclipsed Ava Sigur—again dressed in muted colors that didn't suit her complexion—who simply paled in comparison next to the hefty Viking woman. Last time she had seen Katherine de Messian, she had been chesty—yes—but young and almost slender. With age had come too many extra pounds and too much yellow hair dye. But once she began to sing, none of that mattered. Margo forgot her troubles and her sorrows, and the audience fell absolutely silent, and all were swept away in the humbling presence of the splendid music. No wonder Katherine de Messian had conquered the Opera world like a brush fire. If she had ever been very good before, she was now magnificent.

On the other hand, Ava Sigur had that honeyed, melodious, and warm Alto voice, but in a discreet, understated way. How could such a small, mousey woman have such a big powerful voice and such a statuesque redheaded daughter like Saffron? Nature did work in mysterious ways.

Well, she had seen what she had come for. Maybe it was time to go home. Too many of the duets they had picked for the recital were sad and reminded her of her mother. With a heavy heart, she was about to get up and leave when a shrill voice from one of the balconies screamed *Fire*. Almost immediately the fire alarms started blaring, making the audience jump up like marionettes and head for the doors and the blinking exit arrows that showed the way out.

Margo looked around but saw no smoke. At first, the people kept their decorum. They were—after all—well-bred people who knew how to behave. They filed toward the doors with a certain order. But as the minutes ticked by and the fire alarms were still blaring and they were still trapped, they got more desperate and impatient and began pushing with some violence. Some of the women screamed, and then mayhem broke out. Angry screams and insults accompanied the violence that was escalating, and still, only a few people managed to leave, leaving the rest trapped.

Margo, who was on the first balcony, told the young woman sitting next to her that she knew the back way out of the building. The woman was with a young child and there was panic in her eyes. She tried to get them to follow her, but the woman pulled away from her reaching hand and went to join the crowd jostling by the stairs.

She shrugged. You can only help people if they want to be helped, so she went in the other direction, toward the restrooms where a small door marked *Do Not Enter* led to the back door. Last summer she had performed with the Opera Choir in *Carmen* and a couple of Verdi's and on a dare, she and the other girls who sang with her had explored the opera house top to bottom, discovering this hidden exit.

She pushed her way against the current of people jamming the hallways in the opposite direction. It seemed like the crowd was about to lose their last vestige of cool, their voices getting ever louder and angrier. Free of the crowd, at last, she was about to turn the corner where the corridor led to this almost hidden door when she saw two men craning their necks over the crowd, looking straight at her. They too were fighting against the current of the crowd pushing in the opposite direction. One of them lifted an arm and pointed. "It's her," he yelled, and the two men looked at each other.

That one second gave Margo time to wake up and take off running. The two guys still had a way to go before they cleared the bottleneck of people, giving her a head start. She quickly reached the small door and entered. She flattened herself behind a pile of props in the dark and waited for agonizingly long minutes. It seemed like the men had kept running, not knowing the layout of the theater, but soon they would realize that she wasn't in the bathroom or at the end of the corridor, and they would come back her way.

She looked around. She drew the flimsy bolt in the door, but it was next to useless. It was so old that they would be able to kick the door down at the first try. She had to prop something under the doorknob as they did in the movies. A chair, because she wasn't strong enough to move a big piece of furniture.

She turned her cell phone into a flashlight and quickly looked around for a chair sturdy enough to keep the door locked. Then she carried it to the door and shoved it under the doorknob as hard as she could. That should do it, she told herself and proceeded to find her way out.

There was a minor smell of smoke backstage, but nothing like a real fire. Cardboard trees and painted canvas castle walls came to life as she wound her way through the floor-length curtains and *papier-mâché* statues on wooden stands that gave the back of the stage the appearance of a haunted house. She passed the empty dressing rooms and still found no signs of fire. Those two men who were on the lookout for her, had they set a small fire as a diversion, to make it easier to catch her?

Once outside, she mingled with the crowd as everyone left the theater, the recital now a complete failure. The two Opera singers and the Chamber Orchestra musicians that had accompanied them were huddled in a group, perplexed, guarded by the theater employees that had hustled them to safety. Everyone looked at each other disconcerted, and rumor spread that no fire had been found other than a piece of cloth burning in a trash can.

On the way home, Margo stuck to a group of people who were going in her general direction. They crossed Sky Harbor Boulevard in tandem, and even though Margo kept looking around with paranoia—trying to spot the guys that had pursued her—it seemed like she was not followed. She looked around one last time before she ducked into the jasmine-covered azalea hedge and sighed with relief. If anyone was watching the front door, they would never, ever, spot her. She had used this overgrown side entrance since the first time she had discovered it years ago. Now more overgrown than ever, it would be absolutely impossible for anyone not in the know to realize that a secret entrance to the back door was right in front of their faces. She locked tightly behind her and tiptoed upstairs.

Chapter 14

Robert Has Something To Say

EXHAUSTED, AND GRATEFUL to be home, Margo crept slowly up the back steps holding her shoes in her hands. Since Aunt Tilly was taken to the hospital, nobody really cared if she came or went. Rosa Nesta and Mr. Snail kept to themselves, and the two new girls that came to do the daily chores ignored her. To the inhabitants of the house, it was as if Margo simply didn't exist anymore, she thought.

It was probably for that reason that Robert hadn't bothered to close the library door while he was arguing with his mother. Margo wasn't going to eavesdrop. She really wasn't. Under normal circumstances, she never would have, but when she saw that the library door—which was always, always locked—was wide open and brightly lit, curiosity overcame her, and she decided to take a quick peek.

The back stairs of the decaying mansion, designed originally for slaves and servants, had the advantage of providing them with quick access to all parts of the house without being seen by the occupants. To that effect, clever architects had designed the warren of back staircases in the darkest and least visible corners of the house.

Margo stood in the dark shadows and yet had a full view of this room that she had never seen open before. On one wall, books crowded each other on overstuffed shelves, competing in space with *bric-a-brac* of all colors and sizes. The other wall had an enormous fireplace with a painting of Grand-père over it in full regalia. Grand-père had been an imposing man, almost larger than life, and in his portrait, he shone to the fullest extent of his glory.

THE BURNING FIRE OF GREED

Under Grand-père's vigilant eyes and in front of the fireplace, two armchairs sat facing the cold, unlit fireplace and in them—sitting tightly in aggressive attitude—Robert and his mother were trying not to yell at each other.

One part of Margo urged her to do the right thing and leave her relatives to their privacy, but the other part of her refused to leave. She approached the door as much as she dared without being seen and stood there as quietly as a mouse, breathing shallow little breaths that wouldn't impede her hearing what they were saying. It was not ideal. She wasn't close enough. Whenever they hissed at each other, she barely understood a word here or there, but at times they couldn't control themselves and would shout angrily at each other, and then Margo could hear too much, as a matter of fact so much, that she regretted ever having stopped in front of the open door.

"We can't keep going on like this, Mother. You have to do something about her before she finds out the truth." Robert got up from the chair and paced impatiently. His right hand clutched his shirt over his left breast pocket as if he was worried he was going to get a heart attack.

"What do you want me to do, for Heaven's sake?"

"Get rid of her, that's what."

"And how would you like me to do that, Robert?"

"I don't know. Use your imagination. Or else…"

Aunt Beth jumped up from the chair and faced her son. Her small frame shook with anger. "I hate it when you say that."

"But you don't hate your cushy life, now do you? Don't make me kick you and your sister out of this house and send you off to a nursing home." Robert pulled a wrinkled handkerchief out of his pocket and mopped his forehead.

"Robert, please don't talk like that, son."

"Then get rid of her." He walked to Grand-père's portrait and stood in front of it, subconsciously attempting to copy the self-confident pose of his ancestor.

Margo had heard enough. She knew perfectly well that they were talking about her. As soon as the Regatta was over and all the tourists vacated the town, she and Jenny and the cats would move to the Pirate Bay for the rest of the summer, and she would never, ever, come back, not where she wasn't wanted.

Blushing furiously with indignation, she tiptoed the rest of the way to the attic and found to her horror that the door was open. She looked around in panic. Jenny hadn't closed the door properly and had fallen asleep. There she was, lying on her cot on top of her blankets, drooling with her mouth open, snoring gently. Drat. She looked for Ice and Fenway with mounting anxiety. She looked under the cots. She looked behind the chests and the dusty paintings leaning against the walls. She looked in every dark corner, but nothing. She called and called, promising the magic word *chicken*, but the cats were nowhere to be seen.

Oh, dear. She wouldn't be surprised if the cats had poked at the door with their restless little paws until they had managed to open it wide enough to get out. Exhausted as she was, she had no choice but to go look for them. She couldn't allow them to roam the house at their leisure and be discovered.

She went back down the stairs looking this way and that, calling them quietly, padding carefully barefoot. She paused on the second floor. This was where her aunts resided. Unfamiliar territory. All the bedroom doors on the floor were kept closed, but there were plenty of closet doors and pieces of furniture that had to be inspected. She braced herself. The floorboards creaked badly on this floor, and the wall lamps projected her shadow on the wall scaring her. She hated the second floor.

This part of the house had never really been renovated. The aunts, stingy with the electricity, or just because they didn't like things to change, had never bothered to have modern lights installed on their floor. Only a handful of wall sconces provided a minimum of illumination, barely enough to get by in the night. The wallpaper was old, even older than downstairs, and it was full of stains and worn-away patches. A few threadbare rugs were scattered in the long hallway. To her bare feet, they felt dusty and sticky. Margo felt disgusted. She could barely control her urge to run.

THE BURNING FIRE OF GREED

After double-checking that there were no cats trapped in closets or behind furniture, she headed downstairs with relief. But as she got closer to the library, her heart started thumping. If the cats were not upstairs, it could only mean that they were down here. And they could be anywhere. She was terrified of having to confront Robert or her aunt because she was going to have to check for the interlopers in the library. She was going to have to explain their presence in the house.

She entered the room cautiously, holding her breath, but the room was empty. Robert and her aunt had left the room. She quickly looked around and saw—horrified—that the cats, curious to explore a new area, had wandered in and were happily leaving paw prints all over the faint layer of dust that covered every visible inch of the place. And at that moment they were perched on the desk eyeing the shelves.

"No, no. Please don't jump on the shelves," she begged them and she carefully walked toward them so as not to startle them, with a vague hope of catching them. But Ice and Fenway briefly turned around to look at her—pretty much ignoring her—and then Fenway, that naughty, free-spirited Fenway, who did whatever she wanted even if you begged her not to, took flight. In a graceful leap that Margo couldn't help but admire, Fenway flew through the air and landed, or almost landed where she had wanted to. But she missed by about an inch, and to not fall, she clung with her claws to the books she could reach, and down they came all in a dusty heap that included Fenway, the books, and a disturbing cloud of papers that scattered all around the room. Ice, all excited, jumped into the fray and hopped onto the space on the shelf that had previously been occupied by the books.

Margo wanted to cry. The noise of the books falling had been terrifying in the hollow silence of the big house. Surely it had been loud enough to wake the dead. She turned toward the door expecting Robert and her aunt to step into the library and start screaming at her or something like that, and maybe kick them all out onto the curb, right there and then. But the house remained silent. Then, the wind brought the faint whiff of a conversation from outside. She went to the open window and saw that Robert was talking to his mother standing by his car. They were obviously continuing the argument out there and seemingly hadn't heard a thing. With some luck, she would have enough time to put the books back on the shelf and get the cats out of there.

After putting the books back up, Margo hurried to pick up the scattered papers and shoved them behind the books somewhere, anywhere. There was a small folder with her name on it on the floor, and surprised, she picked it up. Then, hanging on to the folder, she shooed the cats out of the room and ordered them to go upstairs. She was grateful that they obeyed this time, and they all ran upstairs as if chased by the devil himself.

Boy, it had been a long day. She locked the attic door firmly behind her and sat by the window to catch her breath. Jenny continued sleeping peacefully on her cot, never imagining for a second what adventures Margo had encountered while she dreamed. By the street light that filtered into the attic room, she saw that the folder she was holding was full of not only papers but letters as well. She wanted to look at them, but she was so tired that she gave up. They had waited hidden in the library this long, they could wait until tomorrow.

To apologize for their misbehavior, those rascal cats Ice and Fenway jumped onto Margo's bed and snuggled next to her, purring prettily as loud as they could. In the background, by the Boardwalk, a vigorous display of fireworks lit the sky over the bay, illuminating the single mirror that hung on an otherwise empty wall. And even before she closed her eyes completely, Margo was fast asleep.

Chapter 15

Death At The Farmers' Market

MARGO AND JENNY made sure the cats were locked up in the attic properly this time and snuck downstairs while Aunt Beth slept. In the kitchen, Rosa Nesta—wearing her crawfish apron—put some fresh meat patties in their hands and shooed them off, reminding them that Aunt Beth's Church Group was coming to pray for Aunt Tilly's recovery and the weekly sharing of gossip, and they should stay out of the way for their own good, if possible.

The air was particularly pleasant on this Saturday morning. It was not too humid and not too dry. Nor was it too cool or too warm. In one word, it was a gorgeous day.

"It's a perfect day for going to the Farmers' Market. You'll love it, Jenny."

"Farmer's Market? Like they sell fruits and veggies? That doesn't sound like too much fun." There was a lot of doubt in Jenny's eyes.

"No, it's not just that. They sell cookies and juices, and all kinds of homemade stuff. Then we can find us a nice spot to sit down and have lunch. My treat."

"Overlooking the bay?"

"Of course overlooking the bay. Where else? Olde Towne—as the ladies of the Conservation Society like to call it—is like an open-air museum with a long stretch of water. All the buildings are old and crumbling, and they are of historical significance. The Old Town was built on salt rock cliffs to the south, so there's no sand there like in the rest of Half Moon Bay, but the view is beautiful."

"I wish I could stay and live in a place like this forever," Jenny said sadly. "I have no home now, and I have to figure out what to do with my life."

Margo and Jenny walked down to East Oyster Catcher and turned right. Saturday Market was a big thing. There were numerous people walking in the same direction, cheerfully enjoying the good weather. Children skipped and hopped, and puppies on leashes barked good-naturedly. On days like these, Half Moon Bay was as close to paradise as you could get. But not so much for Margo. She kept looking around her in case she spotted the guys that had tried to hurt her. But how was she going to recognize them? She had barely had a glimpse of them. Besides, there were so many strangers in town that it would have been impossible to recognize someone who didn't belong.

"So you don't think that the new wife, I mean your uncle's widow will soften her heart and let you go back?"

"No, I don't think so. She hates me. She's never liked me that much, but now, she really hates me, and I don't know why."

"Maybe it's because your uncle left you so much money instead of leaving it to her," Margo said, indignation in her voice.

"But that was my mother's money and therefore legally mine. He was just keeping it safe for me. The sad thing is that those children are my little cousins, and they're all the family I have in the world, and I'm not allowed to spend time with them."

"Don't be sad, Jenny. You have me."

"Yes, but it looks like you won't have a home much longer either."

"I know."

The girls reached the old stone walls, or at least what was left of them, and entered what the locals called Old Town. This was where the pirates settled down to build their settlement. Most of it had crumbled to nothing despite the rebuilding efforts by the Conservation Society.

"So is this where your ancestor first landed?" Jenny asked.

"Supposedly. But mine was smarter than the other pirates, and he built his house on the sandy side. Francesc Fontayn was a smart man, and the lands he left his descendants are now worth a fortune."

"So you got your share as well?"

"Oh, no. My mom left Half Moon Bay in a huff and a puff when she was very young, and I guess Grand-père disinherited her because as far as I know, every penny mom had she had earned herself. And here's the market."

The girls stepped off the grass and pebble walkway and into a fruit and veggie wonderland. They walked among the stalls and admired the jars of marmalade and the pots of honey. There were women making jewelry out of colorful beads, and painters with their easels exhibiting their seascapes painted in lively hues of blues and sea spray green, all with little boats bobbing on the water and children playing on the sand, or chasing beach balls while onlookers admired them from under large multicolored umbrellas. In a clearing by the Cajun food exhibit and tasting stalls, young men and women dressed as clowns or pirates did face painting and hair braiding for the children.

"And this is the cookie stall I told you about," Margo said and fell silent in front of an enormous stall under a multicolored striped awning. The two girls stood in front of the enormous cookie table and looked on respectfully. There were more types of cookies on that table than had ever been invented, their sugar coatings in every hue of the rainbow, with bits of nuts and chips of chocolate or coconut, cookies sitting in gooey caramel sauce and cookies sitting in powdered sugar. "Ladies," the proud vendor told them in a booming voice when he saw them admire his confections, "these are the best cookies in the world."

By then, a swarm of people young and old had gathered in front of the cookie stall and were standing admiringly next to Margo and Jenny. Suddenly, Margo felt as if eyes were watching her, and she turned around uneasily. Paranoia had a way of getting to you and spoiling your life. Even though she didn't see anything, the feeling remained, and she bought a big bag of cookies, but the fun was gone.

"Come on, Jenny, let's get something to eat and then go home."

"Did you see them?"

"No, but I keep getting the feeling that we're being watched."

They hurried to the Parrot Joe Shack. Even from dozens of feet away, the smell of fried seafood and gumbo perfumed the salty seaside air. Lucky to find an empty spot in a corner in spite of the crowd, they sipped on their drinks while they waited impatiently for their orders. In the end, the seafood platter was as good as Margo had promised Jenny, but they barely did it justice, the conversation constantly going back to the question: what if they were found? Margo's fear was catchy, and Jenny too was becoming nervous.

They backtracked their route, walking fast between the stalls, looking over their shoulders, ignoring the wares. One time, Jenny turned back suddenly and gasped. "I'm pretty sure I saw something," she told Margo. "There, behind the pots and pans vendor." Margo didn't even turn around. She grabbed Jenny's arm, and they picked up their speed.

They reached the crumbling town wall and exited by the large grille gate. They crossed Clearwater Drive and mingled with a group of people walking toward the boulevard. They had almost reached Sunny Bliss Drive when someone screamed behind them. Margo turned and saw a heavy elderly woman sitting on the floor screaming, and two men who had obviously caused her to fall, jump over her and her spilled groceries. In a frozen moment as she turned, Margo saw the woman's oranges begin to roll down the incline and some kind Samaritan stopped to help her up. Children ran down the street in pursuit of her oranges, laughing with glee.

It was impossible to go any faster. There were too many people on the sidewalk. This was Regatta week and Half Moon Bay was full of tourists and relatives. And these were busy streets where cars often drove too fast, disregarding the speed limits. Stepping down from the curb to run on the road was out of the question.

"Oh, Margo, what are we going to do?" Jenny wailed, holding tight to Margo's arm.

"I'll think of something. In the meantime, we keep running."

They bumped into people, and people got angry, but at least the girls were careful not to hurt anyone as they ran. On the other hand, the two gorillas that followed them were cruel and uncaring, shoving people out of their way on purpose, brushing their packages out of their arms with powerful hands that pushed them out of their way.

Margo was breathless. Saltwater Drive was coming up and they were supposed to turn left to go home, but she knew she couldn't risk them finding out where she lived. Then she had a thought. She would continue running until they reached the police station, and she would arrive screaming. Someone was bound to come out and help them.

Encouraged by the idea, she held on to Jenny and made a dash for the busy street. They avoided the cars coming and going because of a momentary lull in the traffic. Probably a red light somewhere. But the same chance helped their pursuers cross, and there was no time to stop to catch their breath.

On the other side of Saltwater, people were starting to turn to look at them, alerted by the commotion. People pointed, and the screamers screamed as they usually do. Margo was surprised at her heightened awareness of her environment. As in a succession of photo stills, she saw the dogs barking at her, and a woman almost suspended in midair as she jumped out of their way.

She looked up. Two-way, wide—and very busy—Sky Harbor Boulevard was barely a few dozen feet away. The red traffic light had just blinked into existence and all the cars stopped. She calculated their chance of rushing through before the light changed to green, but from such a great distance it was impossible to tell. Still, she hurried them along hoping for a miracle.

When they reached the boulevard, traffic was getting antsy. You can almost tell when the light is about to change because people start inching their cars forward. She looked back quickly and saw the guys half a block behind them. They had bumped into so many people that they had unavoidably been slowed down.

She tried to invoke the Patron Saint of safe street crossings and couldn't think of a name, but she yanked Jenny's arm anyway and rushed forward. Meantime, the light changed. The rest of the people who had hurried to the boulevard with them had stopped, yet Margo and Jenny defied the now moving and honking vehicles and the insults being hurled at them.

Almost against all odds, they were now safely on the other side, and Margo ventured a backward glance. The men, perhaps mesmerized by the rhythm of the pursuit, or thinking that they too could defy so many angry drivers, dashed into the traffic and started zigzagging between ever-accelerating cars.

But guardian angels can't keep their eyes on all fools, and the two men failed to negotiate the distance between two cars that were coming too fast down the boulevard to stop at such short notice. Margo grabbed her throat with one hand in horror and held tight to Jenny's hand as the screeching of brakes and a horrible thud accompanied the screaming of the people that realized that the two men had just been hit.

That was not the worst part of it either. While one of the men was tossed sideways like a rag doll, hit the curb with his head, and went limp right away, the other one was a few feet behind his companion. He was hit by an old green car that raised his body into the air where he flipped and started falling. Before he collapsed against the road, another car that had been speeding down the boulevard unaware of what was going on, hit the poor man as well, and for a second time, his broken body rose into the air. It seemed like it took him forever to fall back on earth. He had been pushed with such force that he flew across the other lane and landed almost at Margo's feet.

Margo repressed her urge to scream, but Jenny was shaking and sobbing completely out of control, and Margo fought hard to remain calm so that she could help Jenny.

Even though the events had taken no more than a minute or two, time felt like it had been suspended as the world stood still. Margo stared, unable to take her eyes off the two men as they were run over and killed, and then the numerous cars involved in the accident slowed down to a stop, and all the other cars entering the accident area hit their vehicles in turn. The screeching of brakes and the crunching and tearing of metal woke the world up again out of their horrified lethargy, and the onlookers reacted. People were on their phones to the police. Mothers were picking up their children and running away from the gory scene to protect them, and those ghoulish enough to enjoy what had just happened were filming the scene of the accident and the broken bodies and taking selfies for their social websites.

But in all the confusion nobody saw—except for Margo who was still staring at the dead man at her feet—that a small photograph was protruding from the man's shirt pocket. Pretending to have dropped her bag and then bending down to retrieve it, Margo discreetly removed the photograph from the man's pocket and pulled Jenny over to a quiet spot in the Opera House gardens. The photograph was a small Polaroid of two girls laughing at the photographer, showing pretty white teeth and windswept hair. It was a photograph of her and Jenny, taken the year before. She remembered because her hair used to be much longer then, but she didn't remember the occasion or the person who took it. She put it away in her purse after she decided there was no point in telling Jenny anything since the two men were already dead. But she was going to go to the police. There had been too many attempts on her life for comfort. And enough was enough.

For Margo, the unspeakable disaster of two lives lost right in front of her eyes was despicably confused with the relief she felt at being safe. She blushed in shame and looked at the people around her, hoping that nobody knew the relief she felt at the death of these men. From where they were sitting—almost hiding—they watched as police cars and ambulances came and picked up the bodies and interviewed people. Nobody came looking for them. Hopefully, nobody realized they had been involved. She was going to talk to the police, but it had to be on her terms when she was good and ready.

Chapter 16

Aunt Tilly

TILLY OPENED HER EYES SLOWLY. The sun was pouring cheerfully through the open windows, reflecting its brightness on the white-washed walls and the shiny metal surfaces. Tilly blinked repeatedly until her eyes adjusted to the glare. Where was she? Was she dead? She looked around her cautiously, fighting the nausea. Was this heaven? Her head was throbbing, and she couldn't get her thinking straight. This room full of machines, with heaps of flowers in vases on every table and balloons everywhere, couldn't be heaven. Seemed like she was in a hospital room. And she was lying in a hospital bed. But was she dead and they hadn't taken her away yet? Well, no. Her head wouldn't be hurting so badly if she was dead, right?

Suddenly, a very vivid memory of last night flashed into her mind. She should be dead. She remembered dying. She remembered how life had ebbed slowly out of her body leaving her feeling hopeless and surprised. *I'm dying*, she remembered thinking. And the terrible cold, as if the blood was being drained out of her body. *I'm dying*, she kept thinking. She remembered that, and as she felt colder and colder, the enormous sense of defeat as her mind descended into chaos and darkness. How could she be alive when she was dead already? She moved her hands and felt the tubes and the needles in them, and remembered where she was, but only vaguely how she got there.

In the background, she could hear the coming and going of the nurses, and the sounds of patients and their visitors in adjoining rooms. Occasionally, honking of cars filtered through to her room, and mingled with the laughter of children playing in the schoolyard behind the hospital.

She remembered the party. It was a party, wasn't it? She had worn a very old long lace dress that had—once upon a time—made her feel pretty. She had been young then, and as her memory carried her to the past, the hospital room vanished from her mind and suddenly she was young again.

She was wearing her lace dress. The French windows of the Broussard plantation home were open, and a wild wisp of breeze ruffled her long, blond, curly hair. The chamber orchestra was playing an endless parade of popular waltzes, and the dance floor was full of happy people, twirling away to Lehar and Strauss. She laughed and turned around. A young man was smiling down at her as she fanned herself with the matching lace fan. It had been a very hot night, she seemed to remember. Whatever did happen to that fan? She hadn't seen it in years. And what about the young man? They had danced for hours in the moonlight that shone onto the parquet floor of the veranda through the open windows.

Tilly frowned with distress. That handsome young man, what was his name? It had slipped her mind. But it started with an L. Lawrence, was it? *Pouyaille!* She should remember, the way his deep brown eyes looked into hers with passion and desire. And that night she fell in love. So many times she snuck out at night to see him in secret. Her parents would have killed her if they had found out. Then one night she couldn't wait any longer, and they ran to the barn, and she rolled in the hay with him. What happy times, those. And smiling, she fell asleep.

Tilly woke up hours later, still smiling to herself. In her dreams, she and her young man had danced in the moonlight again and had held each other tight while he whispered sweet nothings in her ears, and she had laughed.

Then, suddenly, an anguished thought made her cry. They were going to get married, and they were always laughing with joy. But Lawrence, or was it Laurent, was sent off to war, and she never saw him again. All her dreams dashed. Her happiness broken. And she never got to tell him about the babies. For a long time, she tried to hide her growing condition from friends and family. How scared she had been. Her sweet babies. Whatever happened to the babies? Tilly tossed and whimpered. She tried to remember but her head hurt. She lifted a hand and rubbed her temple but the hospital machine she was connected to started beeping, so she quickly lowered it again. A tear ran down her sallow, emaciated face.

It would have been so much better if she would have died. Why were they keeping her hooked to all those horrible machines? Why did they insist on keeping her alive? She was more than ready to go, wasn't she?

A cloud sailed in front of the sun casting a shadow into the room, and Tilly remembered last night, and the shadow that came to visit her. She had been feeling better and there was talk of going back home. But the shadow had come and entered the room after the night nurse turned the lights off.

"Are you death? Are you here to take me?" she asked the shadow, dressed in dark clothes, a mask on its face. Not even the eyes were visible in the penumbra. It had to be death. With a voice that was neither human nor animal, the shadow asked her if she was ready to go. "Some days I'm ready. Some days I am so very tired that I want to sleep and never wake up, but other days I want to keep on living forever."

The shadow pulled up a chair and gently held her hand. "I'm sorry," it said softly. "It wasn't supposed to happen this way."

"It's all right," Tilly said, fighting back the apprehension. "Will it hurt?"

"No, it won't. I'll make sure of that."

"Who are you?" she asked, thinking that the voice sounded vaguely familiar. "You aren't death. I think I know you."

"What does it matter? I have to do this. And you're ready to go anyway."

"Yes, yes. But I have unfinished business. I want to tell Margo good-bye. I want to finish my will and leave something for Snail, and for

Rosa Nesta. Nothing for Beth, or for that horrible Robert. They don't deserve anything. I must change my will."

"I'll take care of all that," the shadow said in a comforting voice, patting the sallow hand. "Now close your eyes and dream. It will be over soon, I promise."

Tilly closed her eyes, but not completely. A truck passed by in that moment and its headlights illuminated the darkened room and the object that the shadow was pulling out of its pocket. From behind her eyelashes, she saw the syringe full of amber-colored liquid that it was injecting into her IV tube. That was that, she thought. She'd read enough books and seen enough movies to know she was being murdered. And there was nothing she could do about it. She was too weak to get up and fight, too weak to scream. So she let go.

But she didn't want to die. In a moment of rebellion, with the last burst of energy she had left, she yanked the IV out of her arm and pulled at the tubes. She heard the shadow gasp and jump up from the chair, surprised, leaving the syringe stuck in the IV tube. Suddenly, the room was awash with blinking red lights and the bleeping inferno of the machine behind her that was warning the nurses that something was wrong.

By the time she turned toward the shadow, it was gone, and she felt herself plummeting into oblivion. I didn't pull it out on time, was her last thought, and now I'm going to die anyway.

But here she was, still alive, refusing to die. She just had to talk to Margo one last time. And whatever effort she had to make, she was going to stay alive until then.

Chapter 17

Jack Is Back

"WE HAVE TO GO to the police," Margo said. "They might be able to help us."

"Help us how? We don't even know who's trying to kill us."

"Maybe they can figure it out."

"Oh, Margo, I just want to go away. I don't think I can do this."

"You have to, Jenny."

"But they're dead now, so we aren't in danger any longer. Are we?"

"We don't know that. There could be more of them. Whoever sent them will realize we're still alive, and they might try again. Don't you want to live? Don't you want to resolve this and put it behind you so that you can get on with your life? If we don't, we'll never be able to go anywhere without wondering if someone's out there, watching us, waiting for us."

"Oh, how horrible. I wish I had never come. I'll never be able to get the images of those poor dead guys out of my mind. All that blood, all those twisted bones. Oh, Margo, I wish I had never come to Half Moon Bay."

Jenny simpered quietly, and Margo put an arm around her shoulder. "That's why we need to get some help. Or we'll never have peace of mind again."

Margo and Jenny walked quickly toward the Town Hall before they lost their courage. They reached Independence Park and turned right. It being the weekend, the park was full. It was a pretty park too, full of flowers, bushes, and benches, with plenty of trees to sit under for shade. People sat under the trees on colorful blankets, enjoying impromptu picnics, and children ran around holding ice-creams or balloons, squealing with delight. The large fountain in the center was on and sprayed the happy children close to it with tiny droplets of water as the computerized water display rose toward the sky and then fell, to the sound of the carillon music.

The young vendor from the Cajun Dog hot dog stand waved at them. The young man seemed to have a crush on Jenny and always made her an extra-special dog. But there was no time to stop for hot dogs today, so they waved back and hurried on.

Jenny was still in shock, walking in a daze, unsteady on her feet. And Margo was doing all the pulling and pushing, egging her on to walk faster. As reticent as she had been earlier about the police, now she was desperate to get there and get it over with.

A large fawn-colored dog sitting by the fountain seemed familiar, and her heart skipped a beat. After all, all big light-colored dogs seem alike. The dog looked at her for a few seconds as if he was thinking. A long trail of saliva drooled down from one side of his mouth, and his head was tilted sideways waiting for Margo to make eye contact.

Margo and dog looked into each other's eyes and with an excited yelp, the dog jumped up and started galloping toward her. Children that were watching giggled at the running dog, and her heart refused to beat. It was stuck in that one thought that this was Jack's dog and that Jack was somewhere nearby.

Jenny, startled by the enthusiasm with which the dog jumped on Margo, stepped back.

"It's okay," Margo told her. "This is Paco."

"You can't be sure. It could be anyone's friendly dog."

"That's what I thought the first time, but now I'm convinced that this is Jack's dog."

"That would mean that Jack is nearby."

"I know, Jenny. It means that Jack's home."

Margo looked around expectantly, but couldn't see him. "I'm not even sure I would recognize him. I just saw him the one time."

"If the dog's here, he should be around here somewhere."

"I know, Jenny, but where?" Margo squatted by the dog and petted him for a while. Then, like the other time, the dog got up and started sauntering toward St. Quintian's Church, on the opposite end of the park.

"We should follow him," Jenny said. "We could find out where he goes."

Margo was troubled. She was torn between wanting to find out and going to the police. She almost followed the dog. But they had hesitated so long that now the dog was gone, vanished behind the bushes around the church.

"Come on, Jenny," she said and sighed. "The police are more important. If Jack is back, he hasn't bothered to look for me. So we might as well not bother with him either."

The Half Moon Bay Police Department was truly small, tucked into one corner of the Town Hall. The girls pushed the glass front door and entered. It was very cold inside. The air conditioner was blasting at full speed. One lonely policeman sat at a desk close to the entrance, apparently immune to the freezing cold. From there, a hallway disappeared into the dark corridor from which a number of wooden doors could be seen, closed and unwelcoming.

Margo swallowed hard and stepped forward. You just never knew with the police. They had once been your friendly neighborhood policeman who knew everyone personally on his beat. These days though, they had a scarier persona, as the news and the social media often portrayed policemen as bullies or as violent law enforcers.

She approached the desk and tried a timid smile on the young curly-haired man sitting behind it.

"Hi. Can I talk to a policeman, please?"

"Sure. How may I help you?"

"Um, no, I was thinking of a real policeman, not a receptionist."

The young man stood up with an angry movement and said, "I'm a policeman. I'm a real policeman. Look at me. I'm wearing a uniform, and this is my badge," he said, pointing to a badge on his shirt pocket. "Now, how may I help you?"

"I'm sorry. I didn't mean to offend. You see, you're not going to believe this but someone's trying to kill me, or both of us. We're not sure," she said, flinching. She could just see the disbelief on the young policeman's face.

"Is that so?"

"Please don't look at me like that. I'm not joking," Margo said, trying not to lose her temper.

"It's true, Mr. Officer. She's telling the truth," Jenny added, her eyes big and wide. "You have to believe us."

"Okay, let's just say that I believe you. How do you know they're trying to kill you?"

"It started at the beginning of Regatta Week, on Monday. It was the night of the Yacht Club Party."

"Yes, that was on Monday. I remember. Go on."

"Jenny and I were walking on the Boardwalk, heading toward the Yacht Club, when this big old car started zooming toward us. It ran over some of the vendors' tables and scattered a bunch of people. Then it headed straight toward us. It never stopped. It seemed to just get faster and faster. Fortunately, two of the members of the French team jumped away from their group and pushed us out of the way. We were bruised, but we weren't hurt."

"That does sound scary, and I'm glad that you're not hurt, but that could easily have been an accident."

"If it had been an accident, he would have stopped and helped us. But he sped away," Jenny objected. "That was no accident."

"Not necessarily, miss. He could have gotten scared."

"We didn't think much of it either," Margo said, waving into the air, "until the singer from the party told me that she had seen what happened and warned me that someone had put a hit on me."

"Hold on, miss. This is getting too crazy. Do you remember the name of the singer?"

"Yes. Saffron Sigur."

"Hmm, okay, go on."

"Then there was the recital at the Opera House on Thursday."

"I remember that. The fire alarms went off but there was no fire. I was sitting here on duty. Could see everything from where I'm sitting."

"Yes. So I went alone. Jenny doesn't like Opera." The policeman nodded toward Jenny with sympathy. Margo continued. "Before the intermission, someone yelled FIRE, and everyone headed for the exits. They became jammed pretty fast so I decided to leave by the side door."

"By the side door?"

"Yes. I sang with the Opera Choir a few times, and I know the theater pretty well. So I'm heading for the side exit when these two guys start pursuing me."

"Are you sure you were the one they were after, and they were not just trying to escape themselves?"

"Officer, a person knows when they are being pursued, believe me. Everyone was hurrying toward the EXIT signs except these two. They had to fight the crowd and shove their way through to follow me. Anyway, I managed to lose them, but they really scared me. So today, when the same two guys pursued us from the market, I decided that I couldn't do this on my own anymore and that I had to come to the police for help."

"Were they the same guys?"

"To be honest with you, I don't know. I was too busy running for my life. And then one of them landed at my feet."

"Beg pardon?"

"They got run over when we were crossing Sky Harbor Boulevard. One of the bodies landed at my feet."

"The two guys that got run over today. Yes, dead at the scene. You were part of that, and you didn't come forward?"

"I was too scared. But listen, there's more." Margo put her hand in her purse and took out the photograph. "I found this in his pocket."

"You removed evidence? And you didn't know that you can't do that?"

"Well yes, everyone knows that. But if I had left it in the dead man's pocket, nobody would have known what it meant. Now—on the other hand—you know that that's Jenny and me, and these were the hitmen sent to kill me."

The policeman just sat there, staring at Margo and Jenny. He looked like he didn't know what to say. Finally, he picked up his cell phone and dialed.

"Saffron, it's me, Sam. We've got to talk." He listened for a few seconds and nodded to himself, and then said, "That's fine. I'll be there. See you soon."

"You know Saffron?" Margo asked.

"I sure do. Saffron and I went to high school together. She'll see us at the Pirate Bay in the restaurant in fifteen minutes."

Chapter 18

Kathy Mason Smiles

THE WATER in the swimming pool shimmered under the noontime sun. At its edge, Tony labored with the net, pulling out dead leaves and drowning bugs with big, strong, determined movements.

Kathy stretched herself comfortably in her lawn chair and admired her lovely garden and the enormous pots of red geraniums that flourished in the chlorine-rich air that emanated from the water. She liked watching Tony work. He was big and young, and his well-defined muscles bulged pleasantly under a tight t-shirt. And he was sweating profusely, and that made him look so manly.

Something else she liked about Tony. He always did as he was told. Kathy smiled to herself. Desire welled inside her like a burning volcano, and she thought about all the naughty things she and Tony were going to do after he was done cleaning the pool. And then, she would decide what to do about that nasty brat, Margo, to make her pay for everything she had put her through. Kathy pushed away guilty thoughts about her cuckolded husband and her unnatural desire for vengeance, and she closed her eyes.

Chapter 19

At The Pirate Bay Hotel

THE PLACE LOOKED DIFFERENT in the daytime. Always elegant, but less formal, maybe less glamorous, although still intimidating if you were not used to a more upscale environment.

The walls were covered with valuable seascapes and authentic-looking pirate swords that hung in exes here and there between them. The white-gloved Maître d' was already at the reception desk when they arrived. He said hello to Sam by name and bowed briefly to Margo and Jenny before asking them to follow him.

The thick tufted white carpet extended all the way to a small private dining room in the back and kindly avoided the Hallway of Mirrors that Margo was so scared of. When they stepped into the dining room, Margo inhaled with amazement and said *wow*. The dining room was in the North Tower, jutting out into the water, giving the guest 270 degrees of view. Saffron was seated at a round table by one of the big windows from where she had a full view of the whole bay. So close to the Yacht Club, you could clearly see some of the sailboats through the tinted glass where Saffron sat holding a fancy drink in a fancy glass.

Sam bent down and gave Saffron a kiss on each cheek, Continental style, complimented her flattering emerald green dress and then introduced the girls.

"I know the girls already," she said and invited them to take a seat. "I hear that the plot thickens," she added with a wicked wink.

"Not funny, Saffron. Apparently, the hitmen made two more attempts on them before getting killed this morning."

"Are you serious?" Saffron sat up straight, and her eyes became wide with curiosity.

"You bet. So tell me what you know." When the waiter came by to pick up their order, Sam asked for a beer, and Margo protested.

"You're on duty. You're not supposed to drink."

"And you stole evidence off of a dead man. Be grateful I'm not arresting you," he retorted. Then he turned back to Saffron. "From the beginning, please."

"Well, there's not much, except that Madeline told me that she had overheard some guys at the Yacht Club talking about a woman named Kathy Mason who put a hit out on Margo here. That's really all. There are tons of Kathy Masons in this country, too many to do background checks on in such a short time. As to the guys, they were strangers. The town's full of them, and since Madeleine can't tell us what they looked like, I have no way of finding out who they were."

"So you didn't find out anything about them?"

"I didn't say I didn't find out *anything*. Although about this Kathy Mason, no, nothing. I looked through old Society gossip, to see if there was or ever had been anyone in town with her last name. All the old issues are online and well-indexed, but she doesn't appear in any of them. As to the men, I've been keeping my ears open. Talk is that something big is at stake, and they are here to bid on it, but nobody knows what that is."

"And of course they will play a game or two of poker in Mimi's back rooms," Sam said cynically.

"I'm sure. Though I can't understand why the police never bust them. Isn't it illegal to gamble on land in Louisiana?"

"Well yes, that's what they say. But we never question them. They rarely come. They bring a lot of money to the town when they do, and last but foremost, they're friends of the mayor."

Saffron looked at Sam with a conspiratorial smile and raised one of her eyebrows. "And Mimi gets a pretty bonus for looking the other way."

"Anyone talking about my mother?" Everyone turned to where the voice was coming from. A young woman in her early thirties—Margo figured—with a golden tan and frizzy hair with blonde, sun-kissed highlights was walking toward them dragging a very handsome young man by the hand. The man looked at the young woman at his side with hungry eyes and planted a kiss on her plump red lips. The woman giggled and pushed him away. "Stop it, Jack," she said and walked away from him.

Margo was instantly rooted to the spot. Her heart beat erratically and oppressed her chest, and she grabbed her throat trying to catch her breath. She stood up, and her chair fell backward, clattering on the floor. The people around her stopped talking and looked at her surprised. They asked her what was wrong but she didn't answer. She only had eyes for the young man, the one they had just called Jack.

Jack walked over to the table and said hello to everyone and then turned his attention to Margo who hadn't budged from her startled stance.

"Do I know you?" he asked her. "Nobody's ever looked at me like that before." He turned his head toward the others, shrugged and laughed. But nobody else was laughing. They were all surprised.

It was Jenny who finally talked.

"You're Jack, right?"

"Um, yes."

"Do you have a dog named Paco?"

"Well yes," he answered Jenny. He looked bewildered but it seemed like the fog was beginning to lift in his mind. He turned suddenly toward Margo and grabbed her by the arms. "*Sacrebleu*, you're the Fontaine kid, aren't you? Yes, now I recognize you. What are you doing standing there staring at me like you'd seen a ghost?"

"There for a second, I thought I had. Actually, I wasn't sure I'd recognize you if I ever saw you again, but there you are, and she called you Jack, and I just couldn't believe that it's you. You said you would, but you never came."

"What do you mean?"

"You never came. I showed up every year on June the 1st but you never came."

"Oh, that. Sorry about that. You see, June the 1st was a terrible date. I should have known better. I was going to school and that was always exam week."

Margo didn't know if she should feel happy at seeing Jack or hurt because of the years of neglect.

"Come on, Fontaine, don't look so glum," he told her and gave her a vigorous pat on the back. "It's wonderful seeing you again. You look good: all grown up. And who's your friend? And what are you doing here with *my* friends?"

Suddenly, everyone was talking at the same time. Margo tried to keep up. It seemed like Sam, Saffron, Jack, Renata—who quickly introduced herself—and oddly enough her cousin-in-law Madeline, all went to high school together. Jack wanted to know what the pow-wow was about, and everyone looked at Margo, but she was still tongue-tied so in the end, it was Jenny who told the newcomers everything that had happened, starting with the runaway car, then what happened to Margo at the Opera, and finally, the way the two men pursued them through Old Town, across a number of streets, and how they were finally run over on Sky Harbor Boulevard.

"Show them the photograph, Margo," Jenny said and nudged Margo with her elbow.

Still in a daze, Margo opened her bag and rummaged for the photo. But she had given it to Sam at the Police Station, and instead, her hand came out with the folder that she had picked up the night that the cats had stormed the library. In all the confusion, she had completely forgotten about it.

"OMG, I completely forgot about this," she told the others. "It's a long story, but Jenny's cats found this in Aunt Beth and Aunt Tilly's forbidden room."

Everyone stared at her. "Yes, you know," she explained with quick hand gestures. "They came into the room—which is like a library or a study with a lot of books, and jumped up on the shelves, pulling down books and papers, and I had had to hurry up and get them out of there before Aunt Beth returned, and when I was picking everything up, I came across these. I was going to look at them, but I forgot."

"What are they?" Saffron asked, stretching one beautiful arm toward it, hoping to touch. But Sam pulled her back.

"Let the kid open it for herself. It has her name on it," he said.

The people at the table became very silent as Margo undid the light blue ribbon that held the flaps of the folder together. She took out papers that looked like legal documents, and several letters in envelopes of different sizes, all unopened and yellowed with age.

Immediately Jack took hold of the documents. "This is legalese," he said, rifling through them. "Birth certificates, marriages, certified translations, land purchase statements, Opera performance programs, old postcards from all over the place, and photographs. Oh, how cute, a baby. Is that you?" he asked Margo, passing her the photographs. Margo stared at the ones of the baby but had no idea who it was. Other photographs were of her and her mother, others, she didn't know. There was no writing on the backs of any of them.

"Are you going to open the letters?" Saffron asked. "If not, I'll open them for you."

All of a sudden, Margo felt uncertain. Had it been a strategical mistake to produce the folder in front of so many people? Now everyone was finding out about her business, discussing it like it was theirs. She scolded herself for having been so naïve and trusting, but not being able to come up with an excuse—short of being rude—she proceeded, and with shaking hands, she picked up the first envelope in the pile.

"This one is addressed to my mom." She swallowed hard and began to read. "My dear Nicole, I haven't seen you in ages. I suppose that by now the baby has arrived and you're doing well.

"I heard from friends that traveled through New Orleans that they heard you in a production of Carl Smirnoff's. He always did know how to pick his singers, so if you sang with them, you must be pretty good by now. So I congratulate you, and I wish I had been there to see you perform. I always knew you had enough talent to floor them all.

"Not a day goes by that I don't regret having let you go. Not that I would have been able to stop you. Once you got something into your head, there was never any stopping you. But your mother— God rest her soul—would be very disappointed in me if she knew that I let you go.

"Are you getting my letters?

"Love, Dad."

Everyone was quiet around the table. It had always been rumored that the famous Nicola Fontaine had been kicked out of her home as a pregnant teenager by a ruthless father and had gone on to build a singing career that had brought her fame and fortune. Yet the letter belied this. It had been Nicole that had left on her own and had remained on amicable terms with her father. But the letters were never sent, and Margo's grandfather asked, are you getting my letters?

The next one Margo opened was a birthday card. She brushed away tears running down her cheeks. "It's a card from my grandfather, wishing me a happy fifth birthday. I never got this card. I don't remember ever getting a birthday card from him." Suddenly, Margo was tearing open envelope after envelope. "This is for my first birthday," she said with a broken voice, and she tossed the card to the center of the table. "This is for my second one. For my third one. My fourth one. My God, how is this possible? He wrote to me all these cards and they were never sent? He says he loves me and he wishes that he could meet me."

Margo put her head on her arm and she cried for a while. Jenny held her and patted her back gently, but Margo wouldn't be consoled.

Saffron reached across the table and touched her hand. "Listen, Margo," she said. "I promise you that I will help you find out the truth about your family. I have contacts, and I have all the newspaper's database available. And I'll help you with anything else I can. We'll all help you. Won't we, guys?"

Margo lifted her head and swept her tears away. There were two letters left. She opened one of them and read it aloud.

"My dear child. I've given up on communicating with you. You write to me and send me pictures and programs and newspaper cuttings as a good daughter should. And this old man is grateful for your kindness. But you never seem to get my letters, and I've given up on trying to figure out why.

"When you were born, your mother—God rest her soul—and I were pretty old already, and you came as a bit of surprise, you know?

Your mother never recovered after giving birth to you, and she slowly languished until she finally gave up her earthly body. I tried to be a good father, but you know how it is, men don't know much about raising babies.

"The reason I tell you this is because I want you to know that I love you dearly, and even though you are so far, I feel a lot closer to you that to those horrible creatures that are my other daughters. Tilly isn't so bad. She mellowed after she had the twins and she lost them. But Beth's bad character just increases as the years go by. She's greedy and mean. She hounds your aunt Tilly and teases her mercilessly and is cruel to her. Of course, she's always done that, but she just gets meaner as the years go by.

"In a way, it's good that you're far from here. You wouldn't have been happy. This is a small town with nowhere to go and nothing to do."

Margo put the letter down. "It's more of the same," she said. "I'll finish reading it later."

"How about the last one?" Jenny asked her. You might as well open it."

"I guess," Margo said. She stared at the last letter for a few minutes, thinking that it was probably full of some more of the sad ramblings of an old man who'd lost his favorite child. She opened the flap slowly, shying away from the sadness. She had never felt more poignantly the lack of a loving family. As much as Nicola had loved her, there had always been a coldness and a distance in her. She had never allowed herself to become too emotional or too sentimental over anything, except when she made music. Then, her temper and her emotions boiled over like a volcano. It was this ability to burn like lava on stage that had made her such a success. But who knew what demons tormented her that she hadn't shared with her daughter, instead, pushing her away.

Finally, she took the last letter out and unfolded it. It was barely legible, the letters seeming more like scratches than sentences. An anguish grabbed Margo as she imagined the dear old man's health failing, hardly being able to write anymore.

"My dear Nicole, this is probably my last letter. As you can see from my handwriting, it's getting harder and harder to pick up a pen. Dr. Lasker says I should be long dead, but I don't seem to be able to let go. So let's call this a farewell letter.

"It was so good seeing you at last. We shouldn't have allowed so many years to pass by. But water under the bridge, isn't that right? I think maybe I should have accepted your invitation to stay with you and little Margo, but it's better this way. I wanted to come home to die.

"The first thing I did when I came back was to change my will as we discussed. Even though you didn't want me to, I felt that this is my money and I should be able to leave it to whomever I love best. So when little Margo grows up, tell her that her Grand-père loves her and appreciates all the kindness she showed toward him, and to use her inheritance wisely.

"I'm going to have a blast telling Beth that I'm pulling the rug out from under her. I have gotten nothing but grief and unkindness from her. Her greed has blinded her to all other human traits. About Tilly, there's no need to worry. She'll be well taken care of. She is a foolish woman, but she isn't unkind, and I know you have a soft spot for her."

Margo looked up from the letter and looked wildly around. "Give me that," Jack said and took the pages out of her hand. "The second page here is the name of his solicitor and some advice. "The main house by the water's edge needs repair. You can trust the following companies. And a list of carpenters and remodeling companies follows."

Margo just stared at Jack, not quite grasping what was going on.

"Don't you see, Fontaine?" he said with excitement in his voice. "He left you everything."

"No, he didn't. It's not possible. Aunt Beth said he left everything to them, and that I should be content to live on my mom's estate."

"Maybe he died before he had a chance to change his will," Renata suggested. "That happens a lot in murder mysteries."

"True, but he could have been murdered so that he wouldn't be able to change it," Sam said, ever the policeman.

"Yes. Probably that horrible Aunt Beth and Margo's cousin Robert. Y'all wouldn't believe how mean they are to Margo." Jenny was always so loyal, and Margo gave her a thankful look.

"I know Robert well enough," said Saffron. "If I can believe half of what Madeline tells me about him, he would be capable of murdering the old man without blinking twice. But I know human nature, and murder is an act of last resort. So my guess would be that they are lying, simply because it's so much easier. They would assume that you are too mousy to defy them and ask questions."

"Thanks a lot," Margo protested, knowing deep down that they were right. She was a scaredy-cat, hiding in the attic with her friend, afraid to make anyone angry.

"What surprises me," Jenny said, "is that they want her to stay with them every year for school holidays like all summer and Christmas, but then they are mean to her."

"Maybe they do it to keep an eye on her. And keep her intimidated," Renata said. "I've never liked those Fontaines."

"Well, we all know why that is."

"Stop it, Saffron. You have no idea what it is like to be in my shoes."

"Maybe not, but you can't complain. I hear your mom came out nicely in the deal."

"Okay girls," Sam said. "This is not about the two of you, but about Margo. It's obvious that something's going on, and we have to decide whether we're interested in looking into it and helping her, or not."

"Oh, I don't want to cause any trouble," Margo said quickly. "I don't need their money. I have enough to live on. Jenny and I are moving to the Pirate Bay Hotel as soon as some rooms become available, and then we're going back to school. Then, we'll simply not come back to where we're not wanted." She crossed her arms defensively and pouted.

"Don't say that, Fontaine. We love having you here. I love having you here. Right, guys? Come on, give us a smile." And Margo looked at Jack and his contagious smile, and couldn't help but smile herself.

"Is the will included among the papers?" Sam asked.

"Let me see." Jack went through the papers in the pack and shook his head with disappointment. "I'm afraid not," he said.

"Then we know where to begin. We have to find your grandfather's will."

Chapter 20

Jack And Renata?

THE MEETING BROKE UP and they all decided to get together again in one week, and Margo and Jenny slowly gathered the papers and got up from the table. Despite all the promises of help, Margo's heart was heavy. She had built up her reunion with Jack to such an extent, and now she saw him leave the table, still flirting with Renata.

"You might as well stop dreaming with him," Jenny told her. "Look at them. Jack's holding Renata's hand and kissing her neck. I know it's playful and all, and she keeps pushing him away, but if they're not doing it yet, they soon will be."

"You're right, but I was so excited to see him again, and now I feel so miserable." Margo kicked pebbles as they crossed the parking lot on their way to the hospital. They saw Jack get into his car, and for the smallest second, Margo desperately wanted to run after him, but Jenny— reading her thoughts—grabbed her arm and stopped her. "Keep your dignity," she said. "If he had wanted further contact with you, he would have stayed behind."

It was a pretty long walk to the hospital. The Saturday crowds were in a frenzy. Children, dogs, old and young people, tourists and locals, all milled about the streets that had been closed to automobile traffic for the weekend. Hot dog vendors were always surrounded by hungry customers, especially those that sold the Cajun Dogs—that were so famous in Southern Louisiana. The secret recipe was closely guarded by the family that owned the franchise. Margo had eaten hot dogs on five continents and was yet to eat one that was better than the Cajun Dog.

Long lines at the ice cream stalls were filled with children screaming with excitement at the colorful balloons the ice cream vendor's assistant was giving away to those who purchased a double scoop. The assistant—a pretty young girl dressed up as a pirate—kept a tight hold on the balloons, making sure the scoops in the cups were really double before she handed one out to the next giggling child. But none of that mattered to Margo anymore.

Even though the air was festive and everyone was excited about the Regatta, the joy had been sucked out of Margo's life. Realizing how much she was disliked by her relatives was poisoning everything she believed in. Suddenly, she even doubted Aunt Tilly's kindness. This was what suspicion did to you. It corrupted your feelings and made you suspect everything and everyone around you. Even acts of kindness took on an ominous aura, and she couldn't help but question Aunt Tilly's love, seeing in it greed instead. She hated it. She wished she could go back to the oblivion of a week earlier when she thought Aunt Beth was a cranky old woman, Robert an unfriendly grump, and Aunt Tilly the one who loved her dearly and wanted nothing but her happiness.

Well, so much for that. She was even re-evaluating her feelings about Madeline, whom she had found snooty and unkind. More and more it seemed that she was just an unhappy woman in a bad marriage. Without her calling attention to the danger in which she was, Margo could have easily remained unaware of the men trying to kill her. They might even have succeeded. She felt that an apology was in order, and promised herself to be nicer to her cousin-in-law next time she saw her.

With less and less enthusiasm, Margo followed the perkier Jenny through West Oystercatcher, then West Seaside Sparrow and West Albatross. When they walked in front of the Town Hall, they peeked through the glass doors to see if they could see Sam at his desk, but he wasn't back yet.

The park was full. A podium had been erected in the corner between St. Quintian's Church and the Town Hall, and the High School Marching Band was playing the obligatory Sousa marches. And they were pretty loud too. The crowd loved it. They cheered and clapped at the end of every song.

A big sign by the podium announced a Cajun band for 8 pm., and Margo wished she had someone to come to the park and two-step with. But she shrugged the mopey feeling off and continued following Jenny.

Saint Hildegard Memorial Hospital had been festooned with *Welcome Regatta* signs and balloons and seemed even more cheerful than usual. But as soon as they entered the main hall, the world quietened down. Hospitals, churches, funeral homes, they all made people lower their voices subconsciously, and they entered the muted world of the living and the dying.

Upstairs, on the floor in which Aunt Tilly had been recuperating, a small group of people held each other and cried with loud simpering noises. "Look," said Jenny. "Isn't that your Aunt?" Margo walked toward the group and saw that Aunt Beth, Cousin Robert, and his wife, and some other people she had never met before, were wringing their hands and crying. When Madeline saw her, she approached her and hugged her unexpectedly.

"I'm so sorry Margo, but your Aunt Tilly is in a coma. Doctors don't have much hope."

"But she can't be. She was doing better, and she was coming home today or tomorrow, wasn't she?"

"She was, yes. But she took a turn for the worse during the night. They spent hours trying to stabilize her, but she isn't a young woman anymore, and she's had some health problems, so she eventually lost the fight. I'm truly sorry, Margo. I know you're fond of her. She's very fond of you too."

Margo was devastated. She quickly introduced Jenny as a school friend and was about to try and go into her aunt's room to say hello, but Madeline pulled her to the side.

"Hold on. Let's go to the corner. I have something to tell you in private," she said and looked pointedly at Jenny.

"Never mind her. You can trust her. I do."

"Okay then. Follow me." Madeline walked quietly to the other side of the room, looking over her shoulders a number of times. "Best we keep this among ourselves." She went and sat down at a group of hospital chairs close to the windows where the family couldn't see her well and asked the girls to sit down close to her.

"You must think that we are horrible people," she said. "Well, we probably are. You see, your aunts were raised surrounded by wealth and comfort, and that spoiled them and twisted their characters. People shouldn't have so much money growing up. They never had to work. Their wishes were always granted, regardless of what they were. Aunt Beth especially has had a mean streak all her life. But don't tell her I told you so." Madeline smiled and looked at her hands awkwardly.

"When I first met Robert, I admit that I loved the life I thought I would have: plenty of money, a lot of traveling, fancy cars, and jewelry. You know what I mean. Of course, I loved him, and I would have married him anyway, but those things made Robert look more attractive than he actually was. Because soon after we got married he started changing. Or maybe I started seeing him for what he was.

"You must be wondering why I'm telling you all this. Maybe I'm trying to justify myself because I've been rude and snooty. But that's not the real me, I hope. Anyway, I don't want to keep you. Your Aunt Tilly wanted me to give you this." Madeline handed Margo a tarnished locket, the old fashioned kind. Margo stuck her hand out to receive it and looked at Madeline.

"Why didn't she give it to me herself? I've been to visit her a number of times," she said.

"I know. She told me. But this was late last night after you left. I came by quickly to check on her, and she wasn't feeling very well, and she said that maybe they had finally managed to get to her, and she told me to give you the locket."

"Did she categorically say that someone had gotten to her?"

"Yes, Margo. As clearly as I'm telling you now."

"I'm asking because someone tried to kill me. What on earth is going on?"

"I have no idea. Listen, I have to get back to the others. Don't tell anyone about this. Neither you nor your friend. That locket might be a clue that'll help you clear this up. Your aunt thought it was very important for me to give it to you. And she made me promise I wouldn't tell anyone else about it. Okay, I better go. Bye girls." And with that, Madeline turned around and left.

Margo and Jenny waited for a few minutes wondering what to do next and then headed to the group in front of Aunt Tilly's room. The visitors sat together, but they were not really talking, except to mention here and there how wonderful Aunt Tilly was. Then a doctor with a kindly face came and talked quietly to Aunt Beth for a few minutes and Aunt Beth nodded. The doctor told everyone how sorry he was and went back to Aunt Tilly's room. Then two orderlies appeared, went into the room, and wheeled Aunt Tilly out, covered up to her chin in a white sheet that billowed in the air coming in from the open windows as if it was saying goodbye. Margo rushed to her side and held a hand that had slipped from under the sheet. It was cold and lifeless, but she knew there was still a heart beating in that broken body. She leaned her mouth close to Aunt Tilly's ear and told her, "Please don't leave me yet. I wouldn't know what to do without you." A big fat teardrop fell from her eye onto Aunt Tilly's cheek and she wiped it off. "I love you, Aunt Tilly," she said, and Jenny grabbed Margo's arm gently and told her it was time to go.

Chapter 21

Snail

SNAIL REMEMBERED VERY WELL the very first time he was taunted because of his family name. He didn't blame the boys in the school. He despised his own name every bit as much as anyone else.

Snail polished the silverware angrily and wondered why he had never bothered changing his name early on as a young adult. But his answer always came back the same. What was the point? He knew that as long as he lived, he would always be a servant. What affectation it would have been to change it.

He watched Aunt Beth enter the kitchen and stood up promptly, forcing himself to look at her with pleasant obedience. He hated the old woman, but she had his life in her hands. Too old to find another job if he was fired, he groveled whenever he felt that it was needed, and he hated her for it.

He knew what the old bat wanted, too. She had been pestering him about young Margo. "Get rid of her," she kept saying as if he would actually do anything to harm the girl. Despite all the ugly rumors she was always spreading about her, Snail truly liked the girl very much. She was courteous and funny and shy. And they were so cute, those two up in the attic, hiding with them cats. No way. He would never be able to harm her.

Why had he just remembered being bullied in school? Oh yes, it was the way the old woman said his name. Snail this, Snail that. How he hated her when she talked to him like that. Sometimes, while he watched her politely, he would secretly imagine that he was strangling her. She would continue talking on and on and on as he tightened his big strong hands around her neck, but finally, she would squawk and gasp for air, and twitch for a while, and finally quit struggling. At times like those, Snail would smile at her with a big wolfish grin, and maybe Beth suspected something because she would quickly leave as if she was uncomfortable.

But today, the old woman was adamant, and in spite of his malicious grin, she wouldn't go away. Snail tightened his grip on his emotions to keep his hands from grabbing the old bat's scrawny neck. Still, he grinned on, his smile a testament to his iron will. She stood in front of him, holding tight to her walking stick, trying to stand tall in spite of her palsy, and she looked at him—all of four feet and a half to his six feet plus—and confronted him. He had to give it to her that she was a brave woman. She must have an idea of how driven he was to violence against her and how thin his self-control wore at times.

"You were in the army, weren't you, Snail?" she asked.

"Yes, ma'am."

"So you have killed people, haven't you?"

"Yes, ma'am."

"So maybe you could kill Margo for me, couldn't you? I could pay you a nice bonus."

"You do understand, ma'am," he said, thinking that the old bat had a very good idea of what all he was capable of doing, "that I can't go on killing people just like that. It's against the law. Besides, young Margo surely doesn't deserve to be murdered."

"I don't really care what you think. I need her out of the way. And quit calling her *young Margo*. She's nothing more than a nuisance."

"Yes, ma'am," he would say, knowing that they would have this conversation many more times.

"You would have to make it look like an accident. Throw her down the stairs or something."

"That sounds rather cruel and unnecessary, ma'am. She's not a bad kid." Snail laughed to himself all the while making sure that his smile never wavered. He loved to see the old bat lose her temper, and nothing made her lose it faster than being opposed in something she wanted.

"Nonsense, Snail." The old woman banged her walking stick on the floor in a fit of temper. "If we don't get rid of her, we might end up losing this posh life we have, and you'll find yourself jobless on the street just like I will."

"Yes ma'am. I'll think about it."

"That's what you always say. You tried to poison her. Then you tried to run her over with a car. What else have you tried, Snail? And failed at?"

Snail thought about the numerous times he had pretended to get rid of young Margo down the years. He had even pretended to let her drown once when he scuttled her dinghy. And then he thought about how hard it was to keep pretending to kill someone, and then have to save them in the nick of time without letting anyone find out. Like the time he had pretended to run her over, and ran the Aunts' old car into a tree, totaling it. He had really gotten hurt that time.

But one spineless Fontaine was down, and soon this one would follow. I mean, how old was this woman anyway? He watched her talk, his eyes at attention, but his thoughts flew far and away into the past, and he thought about how he should have married Suzette after high school and settled down to have a bunch of kids as she had wanted. He shouldn't have joined the army to prove to the world how tough he was, and he wouldn't have become this lonely beast trying to kill one Fontaine while protecting the other.

Snail suppressed a sigh and forced his mind to come back. "Yes, ma'am," he said. "I'll see what I can do."

"Promise?"

"Yes. I promise."

He watched the old bat leave, all shaky and full of poison, and wondered for the thousandth time why he was still working for a Fontaine.

Chapter 22

Madeline And Aunt Beth Gossip

ROSA NESTA MOVED CLOSER to the dining room door and listened. She felt that it was her duty to eavesdrop. Just in case. Tilly Fontaine was near death, and if she didn't wake up from her coma, there would be big changes in the household. She dreaded those changes. Even though nobody could control Aunt Beth's temper, at least Tilly Fontaine was a calming influence on her, keeping the household from running away through sheer kindness.

As usual, when she was stressed, she remembered Monsieur François and how nice life had been under his kind tutelage. Rosa Nesta wrung her hands. Ever since he had died, the place had become a house of horrors, with that cantankerous bully Aunt Beth terrorizing everyone and threatening to fire them, or worse.

But tonight, putting on a show of love and compassion, she had invited her friends from Church to come to the house to pray the Rosary for the poor sopsy's soul. Which was ridiculous, she thought, because she wasn't even dead yet, and already they were burying her. She saw Aunt Beth lean over next to Madeline's ear and whisper. She got a little closer to the door and listened attentively.

"Have you heard?" she heard Aunt Beth ask.

"What?"

"It would seem like my sister was poisoned." She watched Aunt Beth fold her hands primly in her lap and grimace with a conspiratorial look.

"Don't be upset, Aunt Beth. I'm sure it's nothing more than a rumor. Why on earth would anyone want to kill her?" Madeline was sitting up straight as a ramrod. The cook was sorry for Madeline for so many reasons. She clutched the note in her pocket and remembered that she had forgotten all about it. She would have to do something. But then, she continued eavesdropping on the conversation and forgot the note again.

Aunt Beth was up to something, the cook told herself. She could always recognize that fake-friendly tone of voice colored with the poison that always lived on her tongue.

"I don't know. Maybe someone who needed to inherit?" Rosa Nesta rolled her eyes. There she goes again, she thought. Snail stepped into the kitchen and asked her what she was doing crouching by the dining-room door, and she quickly shushed him. She stepped a little closer.

"I didn't know she had anything to leave," Madeline was saying.

"Who knows? Father was always very secretive. When he died, the solicitor, instead of reading out the will in front of everyone, presented us individually with an envelope. None of us knew what he wrote to each. He had a twisted sense of humor."

"That doesn't sound very legal to me. I thought wills had to be read in front of all the beneficiaries."

"I don't know. All I know is that Father always got what he wanted. So we each went to separate rooms and read our own letter."

"Do you really think someone tried to murder her for her money? Poor dear Aunt Tilly. She doesn't seem to have any. I don't remember the last time she bought herself a new pair of shoes."

"You're naïve, Madeline. She doesn't shop because she's stingy. I'm sure she has plenty of money tucked away somewhere."

"Did you ever find out what was in her letter from your father?"

"I didn't, but it wasn't from lack of trying. There's no telling where she hid it. I looked in her room more times than I can remember. Finally, I gave up. But maybe someone thought Tilly would leave her money, and that's why she poisoned her."

"You're thinking about Margo, aren't you? Come on, Aunt Beth, you know that doesn't make any sense. Margo has her own money."

"That's what she makes everyone think." The cook watched as a sly look came over Beth's face, and Madeleine shivered. Rosa Nesta shivered too and felt as if someone had just walked over her grave. Was she imagining things or was the old woman trying to pin Tilly Fontaine's future death by poisoning on the young orphan? Dear Monsieur François was probably twisting and turning in his grave. She shook her head and went and sat down by Snail and his never-ending silver polishing.

"You worry too much, Rosa. We won't let young Margo get hurt."

"But she's such an evil woman."

"She is that for sure, but she is old, and she depends on others to do her evil. And we won't let her." Snail patted Rosa's hand and fondly imagined what it would feel like to strangle the nasty old bat with his bare naked hands.

Chapter 23

Aunt Beth Prays The Rosary

BETH'S OLD CRONIES filed into the living room one by one, led by a morose Snail dressed in impeccable full butler gear. One after the other the whiteheads bobbed in front of him as he directed them to their chairs, all dressed in pious black, holding prayer books and rosaries. Then, with sanctimonious sorrow, they all sat down to gossip.

Rosa Nesta had made copious amounts of finger food for the occasion, and Snail and the two day girls had laid the food and the good china on a sideboard—buffet style. These were the sisters' friends from Church, and it was very important to cause the best impression possible.

Twelve chairs had been organized in a circle in the main parlor. In the absence of Father Armand, Beth herself decided to preside, making a great effort to speak with a voice full of a sorrow that she was far from feeling. But appearances must be preserved. Father wouldn't have had it any other way. And so at 9 pm. on the dot, they began to pray. Margo and Madeleine—new to the rosary scene—sat uncomfortably among her and her nine guests. Beth looked at them often to make sure that they were behaving as they were expected, but they squirmed too much. She was going to have to have a word with them when her friends left. She read the prayer in a halting Latin, accenting heavily.

De profundis clamavi ad Te, Domine: Domine, exaudi vocem meam.

She turned the beads in her fingers as her lips read out the printed words on the stand in front of her.

Fiant aures Tuæ intendentes: in vocem deprecationis meæ.

How many times had she prayed for the dying and the dead in her life? How many times? She was nearing the end of her life and for a second she felt vulnerable. She had accomplished so little of what she had intended to do. She seldom traveled, she never remarried, and before she knew it, the years had passed away in front of her, and she had become a bitter, unhappy woman.

Si iniquitates observaveris, Domine: Domine, quis sustinebit?

Then, she lost Father. She had never really missed Mother, but it almost killed her when Father died, especially because after a lifetime of trying to get Father to love her, she had failed. Then she lost her husband, and soon after, her rebellious son Chris. And she was left with Robert, unfriendly, unmanageable, boring Robert, who didn't like to work and had no interest in getting ahead. What had she ever done to the universe to deserve this?

Quia apud Te propitiatio est: et propter legem Tuam sustinui Te, Domine.

Beth couldn't hide the disappointment in her voice. Even remembering back after all those years, the bile still rose within her. The cruel, nasty letter was still etched in her memory word by word as if it had been written the day before. "You'll have to beg your children to support you. And every time you ask them for money, remember the times you made my life miserable, especially in my old age. Robert is just like you: selfish and bitter. He will not give you much. You'll probably have to fight him for every penny. But Chris has a good heart. He won't let his mommy starve, if you don't chase him away, that is."

Sustinuit anima mea in verbo ejus: speravit anima mea in Domino.

And then Chris up and left without a word. Well, that wasn't true. There had been many words, way too many words. Beth looked up and realized that Madeline was staring at her. Had she inadvertently betrayed her true feelings? She quickly composed her countenance and looked back at Madeline with what she thought were limpid, kind eyes. She had to play nice to her daughter-in-law, and she knew it.

A custodia matutina usque ad noctem: speret Israël in Domino.

Beth repressed the urge to get up from her chair and walk away. Would she really be able to continue this charade for another eight days? Pretend all this sorrow when all she felt was relief that she wouldn't have to live with Tilly's sanctimonious whining and complaining another day?

Quia apud Dominum misericordia: et copiosa apud eum redemptio.

All she wanted was to find out how much money Tilly had squirreled away, and whom she was leaving it all to.

Requiem æternam dona eis, Domine. Et lux perpetua luceat eis.

Sensing that her guests were noticing her distraction, Beth forced herself to focus and keep reading. At the end—after the last words—she looked up at her friends and managed to squeeze out a couple of insincere tears. She hoped they hadn't noticed.

Chapter 24

The Library

MARGO CROUCHED in the darkest corner of the back stairs and listened carefully. The last of the guests had left—finally—and Aunt Beth was making the evening rounds of the house with Snail, fussing at him for something with that shrill, authoritarian voice. She could see the aunt in her mind, clop-clopping with her walking stick, randomly lifting it with shaking hands and hitting poor Snail with it. How did one tiny old woman manage to make a whole household cower, it was beyond her. It absolutely baffled her. And it was embarrassing to have to admit that she was one of them, one of the ones that cowered.

She heard Aunt Beth slowly go upstairs, her frail body making an effort to mount the steps. From where she was hiding, she could hear the grunts of effort that the old bully was putting into it, and for a second she felt pity. It was her instinct to jump up and help, but that would mean giving her hiding place away, and that she couldn't do. Besides, Aunt Beth would feel humiliated and punish her for exposing her weakness.

Peeking carefully from the dark shadows, she watched her aunt progress along the endless hallway of the second floor on her way to her rooms. The feeble lights from the wall sconces projected her shadow on the wall distorting it, as she shuffled on, at times making her enormously tall and scary looking, at times shrinking her into the woodwork. But finally, the clop-clopping stopped, and the firm bang of a heavy wooden door slamming shut told her that the aunt was in for the night.

Margo took a deep breath and stepped out of the darkness. She had done something horrible on this day, and it weighed heavily on her conscience. She had stolen the house keys from Rosa Nesta while the exhausted cook was busy with her kitchen. But she knew she had no choice. Both Sam and Jack had told her to make an effort and find the will. She would have to replace the keys later.

"Are you insane?" Jenny had asked. "What if she catches you snooping?"

"I have to do it, Jenny. I have to try to find the will."

She looked up at the top of the flight of stairs where Jenny's face stared down at her from the attic landing with panic. She waved and smiled reassuringly at Jenny and headed for the library. It was just her luck that the wooden boards creaked so loudly under her feet tonight. Was it the humidity? Perhaps. But then maybe they always creaked, and she didn't notice because she wasn't feeling so guilty. In the kitchen, Rosa Nesta's radio hummed along with a tropical beat while the cook cleaned up. She did her best to be quiet, carefully handling the huge bunch of household keys.

Her hands shook as she tried them in the keyhole—one by one—looking for the one that fit. And her heart beat so hard, she was surprised it hadn't attracted the whole household. In a fit of nervous giggles, she thanked her lucky stars that Aunt Beth didn't have a yapping dog.

Suddenly, Aunt Beth's bell rang through the whole house like a tornado warning siren that wouldn't stop, and after a string of unintelligible curses, Rosa Nesta headed for the back stairs, huffing and puffing. The bell continued to ring on and off until she heard the cook knock on her aunt's door. Shaking from the stress, she flattened herself against the wall in the dark and waited. The ticking seconds felt like ticking hours. It was hot and humid in the dark corner, and sweat poured down her temples and down the small of her back. Finally, after what had felt like forever, she heard Rosa Nesta begin her descent. Her grunts followed her all the way to the kitchen where she answered something that Snail asked, but Margo was too far to hear the answer.

Looking constantly behind her back, worried that she was about to be discovered, she worked as fast as she could. It took a long time—trying the keys one by one—and she was drenched in sweat by the time she managed to open the heavy door. Then, relieved, she stepped inside.

THE BURNING FIRE OF GREED

It was a beautiful room. Or rather, it had once been. The ornate, carved shelves were full of books, mostly old, and all sorts of intriguing objects mingled with them where space had been allowed to accommodate them. She had never seen the aunts or Robert read, so it surprised her to see so many books on the shelves. And the smell of old age and decay was unmistakable. For the first second or two, it was almost pleasant, that smell of old books, but soon the mustiness got to her and gave her the need to cough. She covered her mouth tightly and got a tiny cough out, but in the cavernous silence it sounded almost disruptively loud, and she shivered with fear.

Margo realized she was losing her cool and hurried to the shelf where the papers had fallen from the first time. The shelf was enormous, and she didn't even know where to begin. In the penumbra, by the light of only one street lamp, the task seemed daunting. She didn't dare turn the lights on, so she used her cell phone as a flashlight, and by its slender column of light, she looked at the books and stuck her hand behind them hoping that one loose paper or envelope could have been shoved behind them and been forgotten. But other than cobwebs and dust bunnies, she found nothing.

There had to be a safe somewhere, she told herself with a mounting sense of urgency, knowing she could be discovered snooping any minute. A will was important enough to be stored in a safe. They wouldn't have left it lying around anywhere, behind some random book.

In the movies and mystery novels, the safes were often hidden behind paintings, so that was a good place to start. She looked at the time and realized that an hour had flown by already and Jenny would probably be worried, and she began to panic. Just one quick look-see, she told herself and hurried from painting to painting in the semi-darkness, pulling them away from the wall to see if there was anything hidden behind them. By the fifth try, she hit pay dirt.

It seemed like a simple, old fashioned safe, but then what did she know about such things? She lifted the painting from the wall and placed it carefully on the floor. She shook the handle of the safe gently, almost laughing at the idea that it could be open. But it wasn't, of course. That would have been too simple. She did notice a tiny keyhole in the metal by the handle, and she quickly checked the keys to see if there was one tiny enough to fit in it, but they were all way too big.

Then, by instinct and by habit, she snapped a picture of the safe and the keyhole with her phone and placed the painting back in its original position. She was going to have to come back and try to open that safe. But tonight, there was nothing else she could do. It was too risky to stay any longer. So she went to the library door, peeked outside carefully and listened. When she was convinced that it was safe to do so, she opened the door and let herself out. And then, with as little noise as possible, she closed the heavy door behind her and slipped into the darkness.

A few steps down the hall, she heard voices, and she stopped, flattening herself against the wall from where she could see into the kitchen. In there, Rosa Nesta and Snail were arguing about something. "We should get her new rubber tips for that walking stick. I can't stand the noise it makes," Snail was saying, sounding gruff and aggravated.

"You kidding me, Snail? And then how are we going to hear her approach? No, no. I say no new tips for her cane. As long as I can hear her coming, I don't mind." Snail laughed at that and said, "You're always right, Rosita."

"Don't you ever dare call me that again, you old wolf," fussed Rosa Nesta, shaking the big wooden spoon in her hand. They both laughed. Margo saw that the crawfish apron was hanging on a hook in the pantry and she quietly put the keyring in its pocket. It wasn't where she had borrowed the keys from, but the cook was getting old and forgetful. Poor Rosa, she would think she had forgotten them in her apron. Then she quietly walked to the stairs in the back of the house and disappeared into the shadows. When she got upstairs to a very relieved Jenny, Rosa and Snail were still laughing.

Chapter 25
Margo, Jenny, And Sam, Visit Lila

MARGO AND JENNY sat waiting for Sam in the lobby of the police station.

"Who is this woman, this Lila?"

"I'm not sure, Jenny. She used to work for the aunts a long time ago. Sam thinks that if someone knows any old gossip about the family, it will be her."

"And she's now in a nursing home?"

"Yes, off of I-10 somewhere. I can hardly wait to meet her. I have a whole list of questions that need answering."

"Maybe she can tell you about the locket as well, and how to open it."

"Maybe."

Sam drove silently. Jenny, in the back seat, had her earbuds on, listening to something on her phone. Margo stared out of the window, admiring the lonely stretches of road, the windswept sugar cane fields, and the abandoned farms. Here and there, cows grazed on small patches of fenced-in land or rested in the shade of derelict barns. The sun beat down almost vertically on the horizon and Margo realized she was hungry, but Sam was in his groove, driving smoothly at a good, steady speed, and she didn't want to break his concentration by asking him to stop at a gas station for something to eat.

At an intersection, she watched a handful of feral dogs chase each other on the side of the feeder road and disappear into the line of trees, and she remembered Paco—that sweet, sweet dog that saved her and then remembered her after all those years. And then the ache in her heart left by the lack of interest that Jack had shown in her intensified. She should have dated like the other girls, but silly her, she hadn't, thinking that one day she would see Jack again, and it would be like a fairy tale, and they would look into each other's eyes and fall in love and be happy forever after. How naïve she had been. Jack had completely ignored her.

They reached a sparsely populated town, and Sam quickly turned off the highway and took a right on the feeder road. There, like an oasis in the middle of a barren desert, a conglomeration of colorful buildings and a small annexed chapel signaled that they had arrived.

Sam got out and put his hat on. Margo watched him as he adjusted his sunglasses and surveyed the area, taking a big breath of fresh air. Then he turned around and said, "Ladies, let's go."

The air was hot and dusty, but the breeze carried the scent of flowers. All around the front porch bushes and multicolored plants fluttered and shimmered under the noontime sun. Men and women in wheelchairs, placed in the shady porch at strategic positions, stared into the horizon with bored and empty gazes and didn't acknowledge them as they walked toward the main building. Only a tabby cat looked up from a stone bench and mewled at them, swatting its tail from side to side, upset by the intrusion.

Pebbles and dried up oyster shells crunched under Margo's shoes, but not another sound interrupted the empty, absolute silence around them. She looked up when a shadow crossed the sky and saw a thin sliver of a cloud sail in front of the sun. But other than that, the horizon was a perfect, blazing, glaring blue. She squinted and looked down.

She followed Sam through the parking lot without a word and wondered what desire to cling to life these people with dead, empty eyes, could possibly have. She shuddered and vowed never to get old.

Sam stepped up to the front door as if he had done so many other times and rang the doorbell with confidence. Then—while they waited—he turned around with his thumbs in his belt and warned them.

"You will not like the smell. You will be horrified by how broken down these people are. You will rebel at the injustice of seeing these poor old folks conveniently tucked out of sight of their loved ones. But you will not gawk or make inappropriate sounds. You will be patient and kind. You will be respectful and make me proud. Understood?"

Margo swallowed hard and nodded. Meantime, the front door opened and an overworked looking nurse opened the door, smiled at them, and introduced herself as Marie. They followed Marie through a long corridor. The nurse pointed out the different areas with what seemed like a sense of pride.

"To your left is the music room. There's a piano against the wall. When we have visitors that play, we pull it out and everyone comes listens. This here is the guest restroom. Co-ed, if you don't mind. But you have to ask for the key. Some of our patients like to go in there and roll down the toilet paper."

"I called earlier. We're here to visit Lila," Sam told her, and she stopped.

"I think she's still having lunch." Then she changed direction and took another hallway, and Margo knew right away that they were heading for the dining room. The noise of chatter and the clinking of silverware got louder as they got closer.

"That's her," Marie said. "Do you want to go sit with her? Or would you rather wait until she's done?"

"We'll go sit with her." Sam had answered for them but Margo looked at Jenny and saw that she was just as startled as she was. The smell of disinfectant and urine was overwhelming. The houseguests sat at individual tables, some all by themselves, others with friends. Most sat in dining room chairs, and their walkers were propped up against the tables. But others sat in their wheelchairs, unable to get up, and made efforts to eat with shaking hands and bobbing heads, food running down their chins to their oversized bibs, falling on the tables, on the floor. Nurses—barely a handful of them—ran from table to table, trying to help where they could, wiping mouths, feeding spoonfuls, but it was a scene of chaos.

Margo grabbed Jenny's hand and with shaking knees followed Sam, who walked with the unshakeable confidence of the man who could take on any adversary and conquer. Margo looked at him with awe.

When the inhabitants realized there were strangers among them, silence fell over the room. Margo felt like everyone was staring at them curiously, and she got the uncomfortable feeling that these people rarely got guests and that was why they were so surprised. She followed Sam as he navigated between tables and chairs, and pulled a reluctant Jenny with a firm hand, determined not to embarrass Sam, who had been so nice to bring them.

When they reached Lila's table, he brought over a couple of chairs for them and ordered them to sit. Then he bent down and gave Lila a kiss on each cheek and told her how lovely she looked.

"What a rascal you are, Sam Stark, always flirting with old girls," she told him and batted her eyelashes playfully.

"Only with the pretty ones like you, Lila. Only with the pretty ones."

"You're a sweetheart, Sam. Always nice to see you. But I can tell this is no casual visit. What can I help you with?"

"This is Margo Fontaine, of the Half Moon Bay Fontaines, and this quiet one is Jenny, her friend from school."

Margo looked at Lila, every bit a wrinkled old lady with wiry hair full of strands of white curls, and Lila looked right back at her. She might have been old, but looked alert and intelligent, and Margo wondered how she had no desire to run away from a place where everyone seemed dead already. She blinked and tried to hide her feelings behind a neutral mask, but Lila smiled.

"I know what you're thinking, child," she told her with a twinkle in her eyes. "Truth is that I had nowhere else to go. I have no family left. And I'm somewhat disabled, so I didn't have much of a choice. My only other option was to go ahead and die, but I didn't really want to do that, so I decided to come and live here instead. Now don't go telling me what a lovely place this is. I know exactly what it is. But I'll have you know that I have a suite of rooms all to myself at the end of the last hallway, so I get to feel sometimes that I live like a human being thanks to your grandfather François who made sure my rooms got paid for until the day I died."

"Grandfather François my Grand-père?"

"Who else? I spent my life working for them. It was the least he could do. That, and all the secrets I kept for him. He owed me for that."

"Will you tell me those secrets now that he's dead?"

"Depends on what you need to know." Margo felt Lila's eyes penetrate her mind as if she was reading it and she looked away.

"I don't know anything about my family. My mom left Half Moon Bay before I was born and she never came back until she gave a recital. The next time was when I brought her back to be buried."

"All right then, let me give you the short version. Then you can ask me what you came to ask me." Lila finished her chocolate pudding and licked the spoon. Then she leaned back in the chair and crossed her hands on her lap.

"I was very young when I first came to Half Moon Bay," she said with a faraway look. "My family was from New Orleans. My dad did business here but I never came with him. On one occasion François Fontaine came to visit him in New Orleans and I met him there. He was dashing, handsome, and had a hankering for young girls. You know what I mean." She looked at Margo and smiled a tight little smile. "And I was a pretty girl."

Margo squirmed and looked at Jenny. Jenny was quiet as a mouse and looked rather uncomfortable.

"I'll make a long story short. After a lot of business talk, my father agreed to send me to Half Moon Bay to live in the big house with François and his wife. It was an arrangement between them. I never asked—having a good idea of what it was about—and they never told.

"The house was big and beautiful. There were plenty of servants, so it wasn't like I had to do any cleaning or anything. But they had a baby, a little girl, so it became my job to take care of her. It was just an excuse, of course, because François already had his plans concerning me, and pretty soon I became the other woman.

"Life went on for a while in an orderly fashion. My lot was good. I had a pretty bedroom, and François took good care of me, buying me nice clothes, and surprising me with the occasional gift. Life was good. At least it could have been a lot worse. But his wife found out. I'm sure she had suspected for a long time. I was afraid that she would have me sent away, God only knew where. I was used to the good life by then and wouldn't have survived in a harsh environment.

"But it was around that time that she found out that she was pregnant again, so we kept the brewing storm at bay. It was just not the right time. She soon had another little girl, and our hands were full with the care of the children, and we never talked about things, never bickered. So quietly, without saying a word, we made peace.

"I was very fond of Madame Fontaine. She was a kind and patient woman, and even though she would have had plenty of reasons to hate me, she didn't. Maybe she knew there was no point in feeling animosity. François treated her well. He gave her all the luxuries she ever wished for. And that was what all men did. There was always another woman.

"Then one night, I don't remember the year, but Miss Beth was about ten years old I reckon. It was a stormy night during hurricane season. Perrier—the butler—and I had just finished shuttering all the doors and windows. The limbs of the trees were banging on the windows and the lights flickered. I remember how terrified the dogs were. They hated those storms. They would not stop howling. I thought the lights were going to go out, and I would have to go to the pantry to fetch some candles, and I held my breath as I watched the lights flicker. I remember it as clearly as if it had happened yesterday.

"Then suddenly somebody knocked on the door. I have to explain. The big brass knocker on the front door was massive. Solid brass. The door was heavy, some solid wood, who knows what kind. Anyway, that knock—coming out of the darkness when nobody was being expected—sounded as if the devil was wanting to come into the house. And then it came again, and again, at regular intervals, as if whoever was knocking was counting in between: knock, one—two—three—four—five—knock, and all over again.

"Madame Fontaine screamed and fainted, and the girls began to cry. This brought François out of the library, and he ordered Perrier to bring the gun. I begged him not to go to the door and tried to hold on to his arm, but he shrugged me off and went to it anyway. I held my breath and waited as he slowly opened it. But if I thought I would find answers, I was wrong. The man—because he was almost as tall as François so he had to be a man—was covered head to toe in a black cape. They used to wear those back then. A black cloth covered his face so I didn't recognize him, even though he did sound familiar. And his hat was tilted downward throwing his face completely into shadow.

"The man followed François to the library with big powerful steps, making his spurs rattle. I remember thinking did he come on horseback in this weather? Meantime, Madame Fontaine had recovered from her faint, and we helped her get comfortable on the sofa. I arranged her pillows and covered her with a quilt I had made for her way back.

"The two men were shouting at each other in the other room, but the door was too thick, and it was impossible to hear what they were saying. Madame was in a terrible fright. I tried to calm her down, but things in the library were escalating, and finally, there was a terrible shout followed by a gunshot. Then, François opened the door with a bang, and he stepped out, gun in hand, still smoking, and he was completely covered in blood. There was no remorse in his face, no fear. All he said was 'You two,' pointing at the butler and me, 'help me clean up this mess.'"

"That's terrible," Jenny blurted out.

"It was terrible indeed. François and Perrier rowed the body out into Shark Bayou and got rid of it. The man's bloody clothes were burned in the big fireplace in the living room. But François was devious and kept the man's hat and cloak. Two days later, he sent Perrier to the Pirate Bay to collect the stranger's belongings, disguised in the stranger's cloak and hat. Back then the Pirate Bay was nothing but a flea-infested hole in the wall. After that, all traces of him vanished. Nobody ever came looking for him. Nobody missed him. We were the only ones carrying the horrible secret."

"The police never found out?" Jenny asked.

"How could they?" Margo said. "If it was raining hard enough, the neighbors wouldn't have heard the shot and wouldn't have seen Grand-père and the butler carrying the body."

"Clever girl, Miss Fontaine," said Lila and looked at her approvingly. "Seems like you inherited your grandfather's wits."

"What happened then?"

"Well, we had to clean up the library. There was blood everywhere. We took the books down from the shelves and wiped them down one by one. The furniture, the walls, the rugs, the paintings, all had to be scrubbed down until there was no trace of blood or scent of death. It took us days. And then, we got on with our lives."

"And that was the secret you kept for Grand-père?" Margo asked.

"Oh yes, child. One of many."

"Did you ever find out who the stranger was, and why Grand-père shot him?"

"I did, years later," Lila told her. "We were lying in bed together, looking at the stars through the open window. He had had too much to drink and was in one of his brooding moods. 'There was nothing else I could have done, you know, Lila dearest, but I sure regret killing the man. He was such a likable fellow. We could have been friends.'"

"Then why did he do it?" Sam asked. He had kept quiet through the storytelling but followed it with great interest. "What could have been so important?"

"Well, it turns out that François liked to gamble from time to time. And on one particular night years earlier he gambled the big house away, the house that stands overlooking the bay. That house was his greatest treasure and his pride and joy. He couldn't bear to lose it.

"The man had vanished after the card game with the promissory note written by François, and after a while, he forgot all about it. On that stormy night when he showed up so many years later, it was a terrible shock to him. He tried to talk the man out of it. He tried to give him money instead, a lot of money. He even tried to convince him to take the Hornet's Nest instead, but the stranger was adamant. It was the big house that he wanted, and according to the note, he was the rightful owner. That's when the argument escalated, and François did the only thing he could think of to get rid of him."

"And nobody ever found out."

"No."

"And the body? Did it ever surface?" Sam asked.

"Not that we ever found out, not in or around Half Moon Bay, anyway."

"So Grand-père got away with the murder, and you kept the secret for him all your life."

"Yes. And the years went by. The girls grew up. I never had children of my own, so I took care of them as if they were my own. Miss Beth was the devil's spawn, but Miss Tilly was silly and sweet. Miss Beth constantly tormented her and the rest of the family. Then one day, late in her life, your grandmother had another baby. It was a shocking surprise. She was almost too old to carry, but Miss Nicole was born healthy and loud. She had rosy cheeks and a friendly disposition. Sadly, Madame Fontaine never recovered from the birthing and languished for a while, and one morning we found her dead. It tore a piece of my heart out, her death. She had always been kind to me, and I had come to love her like she had been my own mother.

"I did my best to raise Miss Nicole well, but Miss Beth, that dragon, turned her maleficent mind to the baby. She was jealous of the attention the little one was getting, and she never missed a chance to pinch her, or pull her hair, or make her trip and fall. That poor little orphan. I knew she was going to run away the first chance she had.

"By the time I left the house, getting old and arthritic, Miss Beth had brought a man home, married him, and had two sons."

"My cousin Robert."

"Yes, and you had another cousin, a sweet child named Chris. He ran away like your mother did. And Miss Tilly got herself pregnant with twins. Miss Beth bullied her into giving them away after birth. She wanted to make sure that there would be more for her boys to inherit. She gloated after your mother left and continuously hounded François to write her out of the will. And poor Miss Tilly. Her life was ruined. She never smiled again. She continued to live in that house full of greed and evil. She should have left like Miss Nicole left, like young Chris did. But she had nowhere to go, so there she stayed." Lila sighed and looked out of the dining room window. The cat had gotten up and was prowling in the grass, chasing something.

Marie the nurse came over to their table and asked if everything was okay. Sam whispered something in her ear, and a few minutes later she came back with a tray of sandwiches and iced tea. While the girls wolfed the food down, Lila continued her story.

"Then, in 1979, Tropical Storm Claudette damaged the house on the Boardwalk so badly that it was going to need extensive repairs. But François was getting old and his heart wasn't in it anymore, so he moved the family to The Hornet's Nest, a few streets over. That house on East Albatross had weathered the storm fine and we moved in right away. And the big house, the pride and joy of François was abandoned."

"My cousin Robert lives there now," Margo told her.

"And now that you're back, you'll be moving in soon, I suppose?" Lila asked her.

"How do you mean?"

"That's your house now."

"No. It's my cousin's house."

"I tell you, child, that that's your house. I always heard that your grandfather intended for you to have it." Lila was getting agitated. "Don't tell me that you don't know about that. It's in the will."

"But nobody has said anything about a will. I only have what my mother left me, and this. Aunt Tilly gave it to me. Rather, she gave it to my cousin's wife and told her to give it to me." Margo opened her purse and took out the locket that Madeline had pressed into her hand in the hospital. "But I can't open it. There's no clasp on it."

Lila extended a withered hand and quickly grabbed the locket out of Margo's palm. Then, she started laughing awkwardly with a raspy voice, like someone out of practice, like someone who hadn't laughed in a long, long time.

"Let me see that," she said with greedy eyes. "This is Madame Fontaine's locket. Your Grand-mère's. I can't believe it. After all these years it has surfaced."

"Do you know how to open it?"

"Of course I do. Look. You unscrew the chain clasp, and the locket opens up by itself. François had it especially designed for Madame Fontaine to hide a copy of the safe key in it. He made his wife wear it all the time because she was so forgetful and he didn't want her to lose her key. He always said that the future of the family was in that safe." Lila pulled the locket open and a key, a lock of hair and a small piece of paper fell out of it. She laughed again.

"I can't believe it. I had forgotten all about the promissory note. When François went to play cards the night he gambled the house away, he was carrying the locket in his pocket. He hadn't given it to his wife yet. It was going to be a surprise. He had placed a lock of his hair and the small safe key in it, and had designed a mechanism that nobody else would be able to open, except those who knew its secret.

"Then he lost the bet and was forced to write the note. He had too many witnesses at the card table to back out. On a whim, he folded the promissory note and placed it in the locket never thinking to remove the key and the lock of his hair. Then he handed the note, locket and all, to the stranger. He told me later that suddenly—in his drunken haze—it had made sense to him because he would always know where the note was, and only he knew how to open the mechanism. And only with that piece of paper could the stranger ever claim the house.

"When he came back on that stormy night years later, the stranger presented the locket and demanded the right to the house. And in that way, the locket came back to its rightful owner. Look. The note is still in it, with the key to the safe, and the lock of hair, your grandfather's hair. And that is the end of the story."

Lila looked exhausted. Sam got up to stretch his legs.

"You ladies have anything else to ask? If not, we have to let Miss Lila rest."

They were almost at the dining room door when Margo looked up and ran back to Lila's table. The old woman smiled. "I thought you'd never ask," she said, without waiting for the question. "It opens the safe in the big house. It's in the library behind the big seascape hanging between the twin windows, the ones that look out to the bay."

Margo burst out laughing and bent down to kiss the old woman's dry, wrinkled cheeks. "Thank you, Miss Lila, and God Bless You."

"You too, child. Be wise and be careful." After a few steps, Margo turned around to wave. Lila waved back, but she wasn't smiling. She had a very worried look on her face. Margo almost walked back again, but Sam called her impatiently. It was time to go.

Chapter 26

The Card Game

MIMI WAITED until all the players were admitted into the back room and then quietly slipped into her secret observation room. She adjusted the video controls and began recording. She had learned a very long time ago that safe was better than sorry, even though she hated snooping on the players.

She looked at the men, all rich, all well dressed, all wearing plenty of bling. She only recognized a couple of them. The others, she had never seen before: millionaires who moved in secret circles of power and control. No wonder they had preferred to remain on their yachts instead of being seen in public.

She watched as her daughter Renata, beautiful in a shimmering black sequin evening gown, walked around the guests, making sure that everyone was comfortable. Not knowing that she was being watched, Renata flirted freely with them, smiling, laughing, showing her perfectly even teeth and her bewitching smile. Poor Renata, Mimi thought, putting on such a brave show for the men, when she knew her daughter's heart belonged to that scoundrel Jack, whose heart belonged to no one.

Mimi sighed, thinking how Renata had passed her thirties and still showed no signs of settling down and having children. It was a silly argument she kept having with herself because even though Renata was madly in love with Jack, she knew deep down that they would never marry. And then who would inherit this lovely, elegant, well-restored hotel that she had worked so hard to build up?

Look at these millionaires, how they moved around the room, admiring the art deco stained glass windows, the priceless paintings that she had collected painstakingly one by one, the plush deep red carpet that had cost her a fortune, and the exquisite lamps, those lamps that she had traveled around the world to acquire one by one, treasures as rare and precious as Tiffany eggs. And these millionaires—who had everything their heart desired—yet admired her masterpiece.

She was proud of what she had accomplished and was grateful for the enormous extra income that these illegal games brought her. As her reputation for keeping secrets grew, more and more gatherings were hosted in her secret room, and the better she ensured Renata's and the hotel's future. What did it matter that it was not safe, that some of the men that gathered in her secret room were dangerous and ruthless, and they got together to gamble with the lives of nations? As long as she kept quiet, she should stay alive.

Manuel, her most trusted employee, moved around the room silently offering drinks and hors-d'oeuvres and picking up empty flutes and tumblers. Finally, the guests stopped boasting and began to settle down at the large mahogany table, a beautiful three-hundred-year-old round table with inlaid ivory, silver, and gold.

Mimi wondered how they were going to choose the banker for the Pontoon and watched nervously as they asked Renata to pick the most handsome man in the room. They laughed when she blushed, but her dear child didn't lose her poise. She answered, "I choose the one of you who has always been a faithful husband." There was plenty of laughter among the men, but three of them lifted their hands bashfully. The others clapped. "What now?" one of them asked. "It seems like we have a tie." But Renata had an answer again.

"I choose the one of you three that has never killed a man or an animal." Two of the men stepped away smiling and left standing alone a young man with thick glasses, whose expensive clothes were rather disheveled. They patted his back vigorously all the while they made fun of him.

After some more banter, the men clanked the ice in their glasses and settled down to play, and Renata unobtrusively left the room. Good, thought Mimi. I'm glad that's over. She hated it that Renata had to stay alone in a room full of potentially dangerous men. She was too beautiful for her own good. But she did add that glamour and that scent of danger that men like these thrived on.

Mimi sat back in her armchair and took her I-pad out. It was going to be a long night. She leaned her head back and thought about Renata's future again. Just not long ago, it had seemed that Jack was about to propose, but then little Margo showed up, and Jack lost his focus. She knew what Margo was feeling. She had seen them together. She had seen the stars in her eyes. And even though Jack had shown no amorous purpose toward the younger girl, she recognized instinctively that Jack's interests had shifted. She wondered if all of Margo's money didn't have anything to do with it. Renata might be a good prospect, but all she would leave her daughter was this hotel, and Jack would see himself inheriting a lot of hard work if he didn't want to go destitute. But Margo had tons of money. All the Fontaine estate was hers, even if she didn't know it, and Jack would live in comfort like a king the rest of his life. But where did that leave Renata? As she turned that thought around and around, she dozed off.

She didn't open her eyes until she heard the shots, muted to the outside world by the sound-proofed walls, but very audible in her observation room. Horrified, she looked at the video feed and saw Manuel, sweet Manuel, lying unmoving in a pool of blood, his eyes closed as if he were dead, and not far from him, lying in a contorted position, one of the men she had recognized earlier.

She sat up suddenly, not knowing what to do. Nobody knew about the secret card game. This was no casino. If the authorities found out what had just happened, she was done, and so was Renata. The police would confiscate the video feed and find out Renata had participated. Even worse, they would discover who all the guests were and would try to interrogate them. International lawyers would have to get involved, a police department would have to be bribed, but the news would leak into the media—as it always did—and it would bring scandal on their heads. And after all that, if one of her powerful guests didn't have them killed out of sheer fury, both Mimi and Renata would go to jail, and her daughter's life would be over.

Mimi grabbed her head and tried to think. She looked up and saw that the men had quietly left the room. Within the hour they would all be long gone, sailing into the horizon. Nobody would ever find them again.

She stepped out of the observation room and slipped into the back room, making sure that the door was locked behind her. She hurried to Manuel, to see if there was something she could do for him. She gasped with relief when she felt a pulse and called a doctor friend who owed her too much to give her away.

While she waited, she walked around the room, shivering from the shock, and by habit began to pick up the chairs and glassware that had fallen in the confrontation. When she heard the discreet knock, she ran to the door and let Dr. Gutierrez in.

"Hello, Gabe," she said, hugging her friend gratefully. "Something terrible has happened."

"You can tell me later. Let's help the young man first." Tall, lanky, Dr. Gutierrez bent down gracefully and examined Manuel. "I wouldn't worry too much about this one, Mimi. His pulse is steady, the wound on his arm is superficial, and he probably just fainted from the shock." Gabe looked at Mimi and smiled.

"But all that blood," she whimpered. "Look at all that blood."

"That's not his. That's the dead man's blood. Look at Manuel's arm," he showed her as he was dressing the wound. "It's not even bleeding anymore. He'll wake up any minute."

There was so much gratefulness in Mimi's heart for her young waiter that she wanted to cry. But there was that other body next to him.

"This one's dead. What happened, Mimi?"

"I don't know. I dozed off."

"How many times have I warned you about these clandestine card games? You know these people carry weapons. It's a good thing there's only one dead body. Do you know who it is?"

"Oh, God, yes I do. It's Buddy Mason. Do you remember him?"

"Sort of. I haven't seen him in years. He looks a little different. Seems like he got hair plugs. He used to be married to that Opera singer, what was her name?"

"Katherine. Her name is Katherine de Messian. As of tonight, they were still married. And now she's a widow. Oh, God, what have I done?"

"Better yet, what are you going to do?"

"I don't know, Gabe. I'm going to go to jail, and so is Renata. When the police see the video feed, they'll see that she was part of it too. And not to mention that when the truth comes out about the reason this game was held in the first place, we'll all be hung from the hanging tree at the nearest crossroads."

"Oh, Mimi, this is not good. What have you done?"

Mimi leaned against Gabe and started crying inconsolably. After a while, he put his arms around her. "Oh, it's okay. Please stop crying. I'll help you, Mimi, but you have to tell me what's going on. All of it."

Mimi sobbed for a while, and when she managed to catch her breath, she told him.

"When we were kids, Buddy and I used to look for pirate treasure. You know how it is around here: all those stories of undiscovered riches that lie beneath the ruins of Old Town."

"Yes," Gabe said. "I used to hunt for treasure with my friends as well. I think all the kids around here did, at one time or another."

"And we outgrew it, but Buddy didn't. He was obsessed. He never stopped looking. Then, one day, he said he had found something. The rumor spread, and now Buddy suddenly had all this money to spend, so everyone believed him."

"So there was a treasure."

"No, Gabe. There wasn't. I'm pretty sure. Buddy and I were always close, and he would have told me, if nothing else, to brag about it. With others, he always came across as a winner, but when he was with me, he was different. I think he knew that I knew that his money was coming from somewhere else."

"Do you know from where?"

"When he was younger, it came from blackmail. He was a snoop, and eventually, he had something on everyone around here. And he had the guts to walk up to them and demand payment for his silence, or else."

"Wow, I had no idea. He never blackmailed me."

"That's because you are the most decent person in this town, and you would never do anything you could be blackmailed for. But the rest of us, we all had our secrets. And Buddy kept them all. For a price, that is."

"But as an adult?"

"I'm sure that as an adult he was up to his elbows in shady deals and illegal activities. Buddy was not squeamish.

"And then, what about the card game? I mean, I still don't know what was going on."

"This is what was going on, Gabe. The world had gotten so used to the idea that Buddy had found Aladdin's Cave—because he always came off as being so rich—that he decided to auction off his cave to the highest bidder. Not only that. He offered the whole of Old Town together with the cave, and that was probably not even his to give away."

"But Mimi, do you seriously think that these guys would have come all the way here from who knows where to bid on a simple pirate cave?"

"No. Not just that. There's the rumor that we're sitting on an unbelievably huge reservoir of oil. Maybe it's more than a rumor. The oil and the promise of a pirate's treasure could have had a big enough allure for these men to come all the way out here to bid on it, don't you think?"

"I don't know. You say it wasn't his land."

"I'm not saying it wasn't his land. Just that I can't be sure because not all those old-timer pirates left wills, although some of them did. Thorough research would have to be done to figure out who owns what, you know what I mean?"

"Wow. I can't believe all this."

"And imagine the Mayor and the Old Families, finding out one fine morning that some Middle Eastern tycoon has just purchased their town from under them and wants to set up an oil rig in their backyard. Anyway, the plan was for the auction to start after a quick friendly game of Pontoon. He said that they would have to wait for one of the big bidders until after midnight, so they would play cards to pass the time. And then I dozed off."

"How did you go along with this if you knew?"

"Very simple, Gabe. He had his grubby hands around my neck. He had bought up my debts a few years back—before the hotel really started making money—and he said he would take my precious Pirate Bay away from me if I didn't do as he said. That was Buddy Mason."

"I can't believe it. And you never told me. How was he going to get away with this? You don't go cheating powerful people like these without paying for it dearly."

"I don't know. He insisted that he had a plan. Something like cash 'em in and run. And he was going to leave Katherine anyway because they had gotten to the point in their marriage where they hated each other."

"But maybe one of these guys did his research and discovered he was a charlatan, and he put an end to poor Buddy's miserable life."

"Yes. That's what it seems like."

"Well, I said I would help you and I'm not going to go back on my word, but I wish I could. This is all too sordid for me. And promise me that you'll never host another illegal game again. Otherwise, I won't remain your friend."

Mimi sighed sadly, but she agreed. "What are we going to do?"

"I have an idea. Change into something dark and comfortable. I'll wear Manuel's waiter's jacket so nobody can see my white shirt. I'll bring the car around the back, and we'll use that old cliché: the body rolled up in the rug."

"And then what?" asked Mimi, her eyes wide with horror.

"And then we take him to Old Town and leave him there. Hopefully, we won't be seen. And then, the raccoons and the feral dogs will do the rest. By the time his body is found, all physical evidence should have vanished."

"The fireworks begin at midnight. Everyone will be down by the water."

"That's in fifteen minutes. Come on, let's hurry up."

Chapter 27

In The Library by Moonlight

MARGO WAS DETERMINED to try to open the safe one more time. Robert had come earlier to pick up his mother, and they were probably with everyone else down at the waterfront, waiting for the fireworks to begin. With Aunt Beth out of the house, this was the perfect time to do it. As much as Jenny had tried to talk her out of it, she was adamant. Yes, Lila had talked about a will in the big house, but who was to say that it was still there, all those years later?

Before sneaking into her aunt's room, Margo peeked into the kitchen. Rosa Nesta was busy cleaning the dishes, her hips swaying to some tropical music on the radio while she hummed to herself softly, so she quietly ran upstairs and stepped into Aunt Beth's camphor-smelling room to look for the key to the safe.

She had never been in this room before. Two large windows with ornate wrought iron bars opened to the front of the house. Heavy curtains kept most of the street lights out of the room but were not thick enough to filter out all the noises. At this time of the night, this time of the year, traffic was heavy, and the honking of horns blasted the silence of the room as the shadows of the headlights were projected on the walls behind her every time a car drove by.

Standing by the window, watching people walk by on the sidewalk in front of the house, she felt suddenly strangled by this world in which she was trapped and yet not wanted. She didn't have the stamina to confront these people. To fight them, she would have to become like them: ruthless, conniving, and greedy. She would rather be dead than be this. To be like her Aunt Tilly: living an empty life devoid of love, all alone in your own age. Where you had nothing to show for all those years lived, nothing but years of unhappiness. Or to be like Aunt Beth: backstabbing, cruel, manipulative, and very much unloved. What did Aunt Beth see every morning when she looked at herself in the mirror? Did she like what she saw? Or did she see all the evil in her soul reflected in that mirror? Was she even aware of what she had become? And Robert, spineless and uncaring—a bully—disregarding the love of his wife and kids for what? To be like Aunt Beth? Or could he not help himself and was simply his mother's son? No wonder her other cousin Chris had run away. No wonder her own mother had run away as well.

So, the keys. Where could they be? Margo let the curtain go and turned toward the enormous bed in the dark recess of the back of the room. Back there, only a wedge of light filtered in from the hallway. She was beginning to reconsider. The will wasn't so important, was it? She had everything she needed. She hesitated. She would rather let the whole thing go now, and go back upstairs and forget all about it. But her grandfather's words echoed in her heart, and if this was really what he had wanted, he might have had his reasons for it. She had to take a look at that will.

She walked to the back, toward the bed. Her steps echoed gently in the penumbra of the cavernous room, and for once she was grateful for that radio of the cook's that was so annoyingly always on. She fumbled for a bit and then managed to turn the night table lamp on and jumped back in disgust. A half-eaten apple sat on the night table on a pretty porcelain plate engraved in gold and pink roses. And on the half-eaten apple—munching away happily on its creamy white flesh sat two fat, enormous roaches that scurried away when they saw her.

Margo quickly put her hand on her mouth to control her gag reflex, and she looked around with amazement. The bedroom was more luxurious than the rest of the house put together. Compared to Aunt Tilly's bedroom, it looked like a museum. Aunt Beth had hoarded into her private space the prettiest tapestries. The small tables were covered with expensive-looking *bric-a-brac* and beautiful paintings covered every single inch of the walls, to where there wasn't enough room for all of them. That Aunt Beth was something.

Margo rummaged in the drawers of the nightstand with shaking hands ignoring her feelings of guilt for the intrusion. Random large keys, spare buttons, old, scratched glasses, and pots of creams, and lots and lots of junk, but that was it. It wasn't until she bent over that she found a ring of smaller keys that had fallen on the floor by the bedside table. She picked them up and considered that at least a couple of them were small enough that they could potentially fit the safe. It was worth giving them a try. She turned the lamp off and hurried outside, taking a big breath of air with relief when she finally closed the door behind her.

She passed the kitchen on her way to the library and saw that the cook was still scrubbing away. Snail had leaned his kitchen chair backward and had propped his feet up on a set of wooden crates and was snoring happily. It was the perfect night to explore in private.

It was nice and cool in the library. Someone had left a window open, and the aroma of flowering bushes replaced the stale air that had permeated the dusty, moldy rooms in the rest of the house. Like ghosts dancing in the moonlight, the sheer curtains billowed gently in the breeze.

She went straight to the safe and opened it easily with Aunt Beth's keys. This time Margo had brought a small flashlight. By its light, she saw that the cavity in the wall was full of papers, envelopes, and a jewelry box. She picked up the papers and took them over to the desk. She turned the green desk light on and began rifling through them.

Not more than five minutes must have passed when she heard a sound, a boom, as if a chair had fallen. Her heart skipped a beat and she put the papers down. She listened, but there was no repeat of the sound. It must have been Snail, straightening out his chair. Still, a shiver ran through between her shoulder blades. But the house was silent one more time, so she continued with her work.

Chapter 28

Rosa Nesta

MEANTIME, ROSA BUSIED HERSELF with the dishes and the past, and it was almost midnight when she finally got the chance to go to the back of the house where she had her room. She was exhausted. It seemed like it got harder and harder every day to keep the family well fed.

The household was still at the fireworks. A good while after Aunt Beth, and Master Robert, and his horrible family left, Snail—the old salt—had locked doors and windows against the unknown ghosts of the night and said he had heard a noise upstairs and left to go check it out.

In Jamaica, windows would have remained open, and the evening breeze would have brought in the sounds of the night: the *chicharras* singing, and the owls hooting to the sky. She missed the sound of the waves lashing against the sand as she closed her eyes to sleep. Dogs would bark for a while and then settle down, and lights in the village would go out one by one until everything but the moonlight would go dark.

Rosa never thought she would miss the days of her youth. Back then, Louisiana was the land of hopes and expectations, and she had fought hard against her fate to get here. But now that she had all she thought she had wanted, suddenly she realized that this was not what she had wanted at all. She should have had her own family, and her own children to cook for. Not these strangers that enjoyed hurting each other.

She had to warn that poor child Margo first thing in the morning. She couldn't keep it on her conscience any longer. There was no end to people's evil. And to think that if she hadn't found the letter, she would have never figured out that they were trying to kill her.

Rosa took her shoes off and massaged her feet. Was it too late to go back to her town? She probably had relatives living there still. She had enough money to buy herself a little house on the beach. Maybe she could live out the rest of her days in peace. She remembered her mother and her father, those angry people who were always bickering and yelling at each other. Unhappy people who took their frustration out on the kids and made their lives miserable. Yet what would she give to have her mother back? Now that she was old, she understood. How she regretted that she never looked back and never talked to her mother again. Did her family ever wonder if she was dead or alive? Did they ever care?

Rosa was so lost in her memories that she didn't hear the footsteps in the corridor heading toward her door. It surprised her when the doorknob turned and she looked up.

"It's you! What are you doing here?"

"Just a quick visit. I have to tie some loose ends." The visitor's smile was empty of warmth and the eyes were cold and dead.

"What are you talking about? You shouldn't be back here." Suddenly Rosa had a bad feeling, and she got up and took a step backward. "Please leave my room. Now." Her heart was beating sluggishly and a sharp pain shot up her left arm.

"I think you know I can't do that." The visitor took one step toward Rosa and again she took one step back. Then the visitor's hand opened and Rosa saw a whitish cord. And she knew with certainty that it was all over for her. She thought about the little house on the beach that she would never have, and regretted having wasted her life so far away from her homeland. That here she had lived by the ocean, and yet her windows had never been opened at night, and now she would never hear the sound of the surf again.

"Is there no other way? I could go away, couldn't I? You'll never see me again. I'll never say another word about you. I could be discreet."

"You know I can't do that. It's best not to fight it. It will be faster and less painful."

Now the tears were running freely down Rosa's cheeks. Her mascara dissolved and left a streak of black smudge as the tears fell.

"Do I have time to pray?" Rosa almost choked on the words as the realization was dawning on her that yes, she was about to die. She looked around quickly, thinking for a second that she could escape.

"Pray. But make it quick. And don't try to escape. You won't succeed. Just accept that your time has come, and let's get this over with."

Chapter 29

Fire!

MARGO SMELLED THE SMOKE before her mind registered what it was. Disappointed at not having found anything of interest, she quickly put the papers back in the safe and locked it, making sure on her way out that she had left everything the way she had found it. Then, she closed the door to the library firmly behind her and sniffed the air. It definitely smelled like smoke, and it seemed to be coming from upstairs. But even at that point, the danger didn't register.

She walked upstairs to the first floor taking tentative steps and she scrunched her eyebrows, starting to worry. The smell was stronger up here yet you could still breathe well. But then she heard the telltale crackle of the flames coming from upstairs and what sounded like small explosions, and she looked up. A cloud of heavy smoke was pouring out of the attic, spreading to the hallway and the top of the stairs like a creeping beast, clinging to the ceiling, obscuring the top floor from her view. She ran upstairs, taking the rungs two by two and saw with mounting horror that the smoke was coming from her room and that her door was wide open.

Her first thought was Jenny; her second, the cats. But she was confused. Jenny must have left the door open when she fled and they took off. Then where could they be? She hadn't passed either Jenny or her cats on the stairwell. Could they be trapped inside?

She waved aside the smoke, coughing and gulping for air. She should run into the room and make sure Jenny had left. But she hung back. She was terrified of that putrid black smoke pouring out of there.

THE BURNING FIRE OF GREED

She was wasting precious moments hesitating, trying to think about what to do. Already the upstairs was engulfed in heavy smoke. It was now everywhere. The flames, still contained in her room, hadn't reached the landing yet, but she could already see them licking voraciously at the lintel. The door, torn off by the blaze now hung on half a hinge. That whole side of her attic room was fast becoming a wall of fire. She had to do something before it spread to the whole floor. If she was going to go in there, it had to be now. Just a quick peek to check on Jenny and then get out of there. But she had to do it now.

She took a few hesitant steps toward her room, leaning against the waves of heat that were trying to push her away. It felt like sticking your face into a hot gas oven, the shock of being hit by the heat. It burned the skin on her face and her neck, but she took another few steps, fighting the urge to run away, and it was only the worry about Jenny and her cats that kept her going.

With her eyes burning from the heat and the heavy black smoke, she could barely see anything. As she struggled against her mounting panic and her need for breathable air, she lost her balance, tripped on something, and fell on hands and knees.

She yelped in pain and looked down to find out that she had stumbled on a pair of legs. She blinked hard and waved away a gust of smoke that obscured her view. Right in front of her, on the floor—where the smoke was scarcer—she could see the outline of a body stretched out with a huge dark stain on the front of its shirt, moaning softly. She inched closer on her hands and knees. If she hadn't tripped over him and fallen at that moment, she would have missed Snail, lying on his back, clutching what looked like a knife sticking out of his chest.

Margo instinctively took her jacket off and rolled it up. She leaned closer to Snail and put it gently under his head. Her heart was thumping hard, fighting the shock and the urge to flee, but she reached out for his shaking hand and held it. She looked at him, trying to understand what was going on. The eyes of the old butler were hazy and full of fear. A single tear was running down the corner of his cheek.

"Mr. Snail, what happened?" she asked, wiping the sad tear away with gentle fingers. "Who did this to you? Let me get this knife out of your chest."

"No, no, Miss, don't do that. Just get out of here."

"I'm not going to leave you behind. Let me help you downstairs. The house is on fire."

"No time, young Margo. Too late for me. Miss Jenny is dead. He killed her." Snail coughed and a spurt of foamy blood came out of his mouth. He lifted a weak arm and tried to wipe away the blood, but smeared it on his cheek instead. Margo could barely hear him speak. She cleaned his cheek with the edge of her shirt and leaned closer to the old butler.

"Who killed her?" she asked, squeezing his hand to try to keep it from shaking so much.

"I don't know. I think it was a man. Wearing a mask. Tall. Strong, very strong. I tried to stop him. I thought it was you sitting on the floor lighting candles. But then he stabbed her and she fell, and I saw it wasn't you but Miss Jenny. Poor Miss Jenny. But at least it wasn't you. You have to get away."

"Please, Mr. Snail, please don't die on me. Please let me help you go downstairs. You'll get well. We'll call an ambulance and they will save you."

"You're a kind girl, young Margo. I'm sorry to have to let you down, but I can't get up, not anymore."

Margo was in despair. She wanted to shake the stubborn old man. Make him understand that they had to get out of there. She started to get up from her knees, to pull him toward the stairs, but Snail, guessing what she was trying to do, squeezed her hand and told her, "It's too late to help me or Miss Jenny, but you can save the cats. Go find them. But you must hurry up. They must be so scared. Go."

"No, Mr. Snail," Margo cried, choking on the anguish and the thick smoke, tears running uncontrolled down her cheeks. "Please don't die." But the old butler smiled at her for a second and then closed his eyes. "Please open your eyes, Mr. Snail. Please don't die." Margo shook him and shook him, trying to make him open his eyes again. But he never did. He became still and quiet, and his hand stopped clutching her own hand, and at that moment Margo knew he was gone. Mr. Snail was dead.

By now the flames had turned into a blaze. She let go of Snail's limp hand and got up, realizing how much harder it was to breathe when she was standing. She scrambled to her room, avoiding the lintel in flames and looked for Jenny's body through the smoke. Adrenaline was pumping through her now, and the need for survival. The old butler's death had provided the shock she had needed to take action.

Jenny's body lay in the center of the room, by the big wooden chest they had pulled there to use as a table. The pillows around the chest were in flames, but the blaze hadn't touched Jenny yet. She ran to her and started pulling her, coughing and choking, and then pulling again, hoping that she wasn't dead and that she could get her to a safe place and revive her. But it was impossible.

Despite her heightened strength and determination, suddenly, Jenny had become so heavy that she had barely managed to pull her body a handful of inches when she finally had to give up. Jenny was dead and was impossible to move any further. And the smoke was unbearable. It filled her lungs and burned in them like live fire. Every time she coughed, she got less oxygen. And the situation had escalated. Margo looked around, frustrated, and realized that she was practically surrounded by the flames and she would never manage to get out. It was too late. In moving around she had lost her bearings and with smoke and flames everywhere, she no longer knew which way was the way out.

When she heard the crying, she remembered the cats. In all this, she hadn't even given them a second thought. Poor little cats. There they were, crying, rubbing against her legs, and she looked at them with sadness. Poor little Ice and Fenway, trapped like her, with no way out.

She fell on her knees, expecting that this was the end, ready to hold them to her chest, to comfort them in their inevitable death, but they didn't seem one bit scared. They just kept going back and forth, not letting her hold them, rubbing against her, looking poignantly straight at her, as if trying to get her to understand them. And in the profound awareness of that moment, thinking herself doomed, one step away from certain death, she remembered stories of animals helping people out of burning buildings and realized that that was what they were trying to do. As soon as she began to follow them on her hands and knees, the cats headed with certainty to the door. It was easier to breathe too, so low to the ground, so she crawled behind them until they were all safely— amazingly—on the landing, and out of harm's way.

But the whole place had become an inferno. The loud crackling of the fire mingled with the burst of small explosions as the flames devoured the rotting wood. It was terrifying to hear. She briefly thought about Snail, and Jenny, and about her few belongings swallowed up by the blaze. But there wasn't time to think. The thick black smoke was spreading almost faster than they could outrun it, and run they did, as fast as they never had, as fast as the wind. On the second floor, the aunts' floor, Margo looked back for a second. The fire hadn't reached there yet, but the smoke was coming. The smoke and the sound of the crackling fire, spreading, coming to eat up everything voraciously, to consume Aunt Beth's treasures. Her paintings, her tapestries, and all her secrets, everything she had hoarded greedily into her room, it would all be burning within minutes. So, following the cats in their escape, Margo flew on, navigating the warren of tight back stairs and hallways through the enormous old house.

By the time that Margo and the cats made it to the bottom of the stairs, the whole house seemed to be burning as if gasoline had been poured on it. It was an old house after all, and old houses burn fast. All the books in the library, the old rugs, the rotting furniture, shoes, clothes, secrets, everything, everything gone up in flames. But Margo and the cats ran on. The dizzying stench of the burning wood and fabric was unbearable and followed them without mercy. It was an evil smell that climbed up into your nostrils and your lungs and made you want to puke. Margo couldn't get out of there fast enough.

She never looked back to see if the fire was catching up with them or not. She ran straight to the back entrance, picked up her car keys from the dish on the table by the door, and grabbed the two cats. They made it outside in time to hear the infernal sound of the house collapsing on itself and go up in a burning blaze like a bonfire. She kept running along the honeysuckle fence, getting scratched by the azalea bushes. She never stopped. She never stopped holding the two cats in her arms either. She never faltered until she was standing next to her car.

Then she finally took a deep breath of fresh air and thanked Saint Florian, the patron saint of chimney sweeps and firefighters. They were safe. It was a miracle, not only that the cats had come back for her, to show her the way out, but that they had allowed her—almost a stranger—to pick them up and carry them outside. They were now sitting in the back seat of her car, placidly watching the fire, somehow knowing that they were safe.

Margo looked up at the sky and realized that even though she felt like the whole thing had lasted for hours, it had barely been a few minutes. Because it was right on midnight, and the fireworks had just begun. And they were the most beautiful she'd ever seen.

She stood still for a couple of minutes looking up at the sky— heartbroken but so thankful—admiring all those beautiful, colorful fireworks with their delicate designs reaching higher and higher, trying to touch the heavens. In contrast, the angry red, orange and black of the fire that had devoured two people she had been fond of, raged against the cool darkness of the night, and she had a moment of clarity when she realized that a new chapter of her life had begun.

It was then that she remembered Rosa Nesta, the cook.

Chapter 30
Jenny Is Dead

SAM HELD HER TIGHT while she cried. In a small town, with only a handful of policemen, Sam had been one of the first on the scene. He recognized the house immediately and looked around for any survivors, spotting Margo standing by her car out by the honeysuckle vine, staring at the burning house in shock. He walked over quickly and saw that she was okay, shivering in spite of the heat. Jenny's cats—the famous cats that had found her grandfather's letters—stood locked up safely inside the car, their front paws on the window sill, staring with big wide eyes at what had been their home for the last few weeks. In the distance, the wailing of the fire trucks got louder and louder as they approached the intersection. He put a soft drink in her hand and ordered her to drink.

"What happened, Margo?" he asked, rubbing some of the soot off her face with his handkerchief.

"I was in the library looking for the will when I smelled the smoke. I ran upstairs and found Mr. Snail, the butler, with a knife in his chest." Margo started crying again, and then she coughed, and Sam patted her back and waited for her to calm down. "He told me that he had followed an intruder upstairs and saw him stab Jenny. He said that he had tried to protect her but he was too strong. Then the man attacked him and stabbed him too. And Mr. Snail died in my arms. I ran into the attic to help Jenny."

"You shouldn't have gone back. You too could have died," Sam said, angrily. It was the dumbest thing to venture inside a burning building. That was how most civilians died, trying to rescue a loved one.

"I know, but I was going to pull her out. Maybe she wasn't dead. But I couldn't. She was too heavy, and the flames were getting too close. He killed her, Sam, and he probably killed her by mistake."

"What do you mean?"

"That someone has been after me since I came back to Half Moon Bay. You know that. Nobody hated Jenny. It was me they were trying to kill."

"But those two men died when they got run over on Sky Harbor Boulevard."

"I know, I know. But whoever sent them must have wanted me dead real bad and sent others to finish the job. Remember that picture of me and Jenny? They picked the wrong girl, Sam. And they murdered Jenny instead. And all because of a mistake."

"Was there anyone else in the house?"

"Yes. I think the cook was in her room. She was old. She didn't like to go out at night. But I didn't remember her until the cats and I came outside. I thought I should have gone back to check on her, but it was too late. I would have never made it back. The whole house was on fire. I was too scared." Margo told him about how sweet the cook was, and how kind she had been to her and to Jenny, and she started crying again.

Sam patted her back and tried to console her, but he knew how she felt, and nothing but time was going to cure that. Margo was going to have to live with her regrets until she worked them out for herself. And if Rosa Nesta indeed got trapped inside, well, they would find her remains sooner or later.

"She could have been able to get out on time," he told her, more to comfort her than because he believed it.

"No, I don't think so. Not if she was in her room. It was way at the back of the house, and she wouldn't have heard or smelled anything until it was too late. And the outside doors would have been too far to reach."

"Let's not jump to conclusions. Maybe she wasn't even home at all. Maybe she's down by the water celebrating with everyone else. I'll send someone to look for her."

Agnes Makóczy

The fireworks had ended and Sam looked up at the sky, at the remnants of the flames—now much subsided—and saw the newscasters' drone flying above his head in a circle, filming the Regatta festivities, and now the fire for the Bay Gazette. And then he had an idea.

"Don't cry anymore, Margo. I think I can find out who the intruder was. I'll find out who did this to Jenny and to old Snail."

Chapter 31
Aunt Beth Has A Fit

ROBERT BROUGHT HER HOME in a taxi, and she clop-clopped with her walking stick as close to the fire as she dared, and she let out a string of insults toward God, destiny, and the fire department as the world had never heard. When she was angry, Aunt Beth had the foulest mouth in Half Moon Bay.

When Madeline got out of the taxi, she ran to Margo and pushed Sam aside and took Margo—still shivering—into her arms. She placed her own coat on her and walked her over to the part of the garden still intact where a stone bench looked upon the corner of Albatross and Salt Water. Here—away from the wind that carried the stench of the fire—the two young women sat quietly and watched the firefighters do their best to tame the beast and keep the flames from jumping to the house next door.

Some of the neighbors came out to watch the firefighters work. Margo noticed that the friendly neighbor had come out of his house as well. After leaving the big dog safely behind the fence, he approached the burning house and just stood there on the street, looking on with tears in his eyes. Her heart went out to him. Maybe they were both wrong and Rosa Nesta was somewhere at the market or down by the fireworks and would walk cheerfully back into their lives any minute now. But somehow she doubted it. Rosa Nesta was dead, and she would never see her again.

A fresh flood of tears filled her eyes and poured down her cheeks. She wanted to be left alone so she could sink into her own thoughts, but

Madeline wouldn't let her. She bombarded her with questions. She insisted that she look at her and answer her. Over and over again.

Margo repeated the story mechanically and kept asking *why, why,* when she knew that Madeline had no answers either. But Madeline was kind and motherly and held her tight until she got a better grip on herself.

Meantime, Aunt Beth had stopped her invectives and Robert managed to pull her away from the fire. Then it dawned on Margo that Aunt Beth was homeless and would have to move in with Robert and his family. And when Aunt Tilly awoke from her coma—if she ever did— she would move in with them as well.

Suddenly, she was very sorry for Madeline, who had obviously gotten a raw deal in marrying her cousin and would now be stuck with two unkind elderly relatives. Because maybe Aunt Tilly was not evil like Aunt Beth, but she rarely showed any regards for anyone's feelings, except occasionally for Margo's.

Then she felt sorry for her own self, and new tears filled her eyes. She was homeless too, now, and she had two orphan cats to worry about as well. She figured she could spend the night in her car, and Sunday night as well, and by Monday morning tourists would begin vacating the hotels and bed-and-breakfasts, and she would find a room to stay in until she figured out her grandfather's will.

There was an anger beginning to well up inside her. Whether this all had to do with the will, or with the skeletons in her family's closet, she didn't care anymore. She was sick and tired of being hounded, of being scared by ghosts in the dark. She'd had enough. She was going to find out what on earth was going on, and she was going to put a stop to all this madness. Then, she would leave town with the cats, and she would never come back to Half Moon Bay ever, ever again.

Chapter 32

Margo Inherits Two Cats

MEANTIME, half the town had walked over to the fire to gawk. They stood in the shadows, their faces illuminated randomly by the red and orange bursts from the dying house. Embers flew up high into the sky and the people, mesmerized, followed them with wide eyes as they dispersed in the cool evening breeze.

Cars were directed away from the scene by the police, and eventually, barricades were put in place to keep the nosy drivers out. Amazing how humanity tended to flock to disaster scenes. It was almost a mob scene when one white Mercedes was allowed through the barricade, and people began yelling in protest, trying to push against the police. Others stood back and filmed the scene or took photographs.

Margo shuddered in disgust. She watched uncaringly how the Mercedes approached the house and parked on the safe side of the street, and one tall, well-dressed woman stepped out of it and began walking toward her. She took long, quick, urgent steps toward the stone bench, and when the woman stepped out of the shadows, Margo recognized Saffron, Madeline's and Sam's friend, with a very worried look on her beautiful face.

"Sam called me," she said. She bent down and gave Madeline a hug. "You okay?" she asked her friend. "You weren't here when it started, were you?"

"No. We were bringing Aunt Beth home after the fireworks. It seemed like the whole street was on fire. But it was only their house that was burning."

"Does anyone know how it started?"

"From what Margo has told me, she was downstairs when she smelled the smoke. She ran upstairs and found the butler dead. And someone was lighting candles. She's in shock and she isn't making much sense. But it's easy to see how a candle that fell on a piece of rotting cloth or dried wood would have started the fire in such an old house."

Saffron nodded to herself. "So now that your aunts are homeless, you'll be stuck with them, I presume."

"You presume right. I might just grab my kids and run away."

Saffron laughed kindly. "If I were you, I would leave the little monsters behind."

"Yes, I might do that. But seriously, I can't bring Margo with me." Madeline looked at Saffron sadly, and Margo watched the two women, wondering why they were talking about her as if she wasn't there. "Robert doesn't like her very much," Madeline continued with a despondent shrug. "Imagine if I brought her home, what kind of life we would have—all of us together—Aunts Beth and Tilly, the little monsters as you call them, Robert, Margo, and me." She shook her head desolately. Then she turned toward Margo and grabbed her hand. "Sorry kid," she told her, "but I can't do it. You're better off leaving town anyway."

Saffron interrupted the sad little monologue. "Not to worry, girls. That's what I'm here for. Margo needs a home, and I have a huge house with plenty of empty space. Mom's on tour in Europe and she won't be back for another couple of months. And I love cats. Jenny's cats are welcome to stay with us. Anyway, it's only temporary, until Margo finds the missing will and unravels the mystery of her grandfather's inheritance."

Saffron had spoken without guile, and Margo smiled at her gratefully, but Madeline looked up at her suspiciously.

"What do you mean by a Jenny, some cats, and a missing will?"

"Oh, just that Margo was hiding a homeless friend—the dead Jenny—in her attic, and the friend had smuggled in her two cats that now need a mother. But the will, well surely you know that François Fontaine's will was never produced, and that Robert and his aunts remained living uncontested in the house and continued using the family bank accounts without really knowing what the will said. For all we know, Margo could have inherited the whole thing and nobody bothered to let her know."

"That's a vile thing to say, Saffron."

"Oh, come on, Madeline. You know Robert and his aunts are greedy and ruthless."

"Well, yes. But that doesn't mean they would be capable of stealing Margo's inheritance, does it?" There was denial but also doubt, in Madeline's eyes.

"I don't know. You tell me." The two women had completely forgotten in their argument that Margo was sitting right there in between them. For a second it looked like they were going to fight, but then Saffron smiled and leaned over Margo's lap and reached out to Madeline, patting her hand with a gesture of peacemaking.

"Let's stop arguing, Madeline. It's late, you look worn out, and Margo here looks like she needs a shower and a bed. Let's continue this tomorrow."

About an hour later, Margo was resting in a big soft bed in an elegant, darkened room. The moon was large and fat, and its light filtered through the slats of the blinds that covered the windows, projecting the illusion of prison bars on the wall beside her bed. She tried hard to close her eyes and sleep, but too much had happened, and she felt that maybe her soul would never be at peace again.

She watched the cats prowl about the room, trying to find their bearing. They were restless too, and despite her calling them and patting a spot next to her, they refused to put their little bodies down. The big cat, Ice, jumped up on the windowsill and scratched repeatedly at the blinds trying to look out, so Margo padded over to the window and pulled them up for him. He was probably wondering where his mother was, and the thought made Margo so sad that she cried again for a while.

It was the middle of the night. The excitement of the fireworks and then the house on fire had finally abated, and folks went back home and got in bed. Up in the sky, the moon shone bright and a few strips of clouds sailed in front of it like flitting ghosts. But down on Earth, except for the lights of the front porches glimmering here and there, everything she could see from her window was dark and silent. Occasionally a snippet of music sailed by her ears, and she figured that down by the water, the party was still on. Dogs sometimes barked, probably annoyed by the crowd and the music. She stood at the window for a while, keeping Ice company, patting his head from time to time. Life felt empty and meaningless all of a sudden, and she couldn't find her bearing either. Finally, she gave up and walked over to the bed. She put her head down on the luxurious pillow again, and after what felt like an eternity, closed her eyes and fell asleep.

Chapter 33
The Big Day

ALL THE CHURCH BELLS of Christendom were ringing at once, and Margo sat up in bed and realized it was Regatta day.

She ran to the window and looked out. It was a pretty, sunny day. People dressed in their Sunday best were heading for St. Quintian's, holding their children by their hands, looking determined to get Mass over with so they could get the Regatta started. There was a knock on the door, and Saffron entered the room—radiant as always—with a big friendly smile. She had a large pile of folded clothes in her arms that she deposited on the bed.

"I don't cook, so get dressed and we're going over to The Pirate Bay for brunch. I have to talk to Mimi."

"Have you heard anything about last night?" Margo asked on the way there as she was being driven in the luxurious white Mercedes.

"Only the short news headlines from the newspaper website. I don't own a television set, or else I would be sitting in front of it all day long, watching the news nonstop. I'm addicted. But there's a huge TV in the sports room. We'll eat there."

By the time Margo and Saffron stepped through the door to the sports room at the Pirate Bay, Sam was already sitting on a leather sofa in front of the huge television screen. He had a coffee in his hand and a frown on his brow. In the corner by the ever-present bar, Renata stood staring at nothing, lost in her own thoughts. Next to her stood Jack—wearing white slacks and a blue and white striped shirt—looking very nautical. He was flirting with Renata, or at least trying to, but it was as if

Renata had completely lost interest in him. She simply looked through him, gazing away, completely oblivious to what Jack had to say.

When he saw Saffron and Margo arrive, he left Renata standing by herself and walked over to Margo and gave her a hug and a peck on the cheeks.

"Hello Fontaine, glad to see you alive. I heard what happened." Margo felt a great urge to hurl herself into Jack's arms and cry on his shoulder for comfort, but she remembered Jenny's cautionary words. If he had been interested, he would have looked her up. He knew where she was staying after all, and she'd been in town almost a month now. So she controlled herself and stepped back from him.

She went and took a seat by Sam instead, and they all watched the news. Not so surprisingly, another body had been found in the burnt-out shell of the old house. Even though the reporter didn't say, she knew it was Rosa Nesta. They had found the body in the back part of the house where the police surmised that the cook had slept. Margo nodded silently to no one, remembering how proud the elderly cook had been of her pretty room. She had once shared her dream of going back home to Jamaica when she retired, and it saddened Margo terribly that she would never see her homeland again. She brushed a stray tear away and continued watching.

Then, another piece of news shocked the little group as a reporter was seen walking around Old Town, stepping over brush and fallen debris, describing how some local kids had come across the partially eaten body of a middle-aged man. The reporter walked the area—followed by a crew of photographers—and showed the viewers where the body had been found. It had already been taken away, he said, but the vegetation had obviously been trampled down. And then he swept his arm around the area where an enormous dark spot on the dirt revealed what had probably been the resting place of the middle-aged man. There was no identification on him, he explained, except for a silver ring with some unusual markings, and a close-up showed the ring to the viewers in case someone could recognize it and help identify the dead man.

The reporter continued walking the scene as he talked, rehashing the events for the viewers, when the camera picked up a tall, hefty blonde woman who looked like a Viking's wife running heavily across the walkway that led to the reporter.

"It's my husband," she screamed. "I know it. I recognize the ring." She pushed the group of gawkers that had gathered at the edge of the pathway out of her way as the cameras followed her and filmed her anguished outburst. "Where is he?" she screamed with a heart-rending howl. "I have to see him."

Two policemen quickly stepped out of their group and approached the desperate woman. She tried to get past them and refused to be calmed down, but eventually they managed to lead her away. In that second, the film was cut off, and the show went to commercials. Everyone was shocked in the sports room, but not more than Margo and Saffron, who had stood up almost at the same time and exclaimed, "That's Katherine de Messian, Buddy Mason's wife."

Jack turned at the two women, surprised. "Katherine who?" he asked, scratching his head.

"Messian. The Opera singer," Saffron said. "The very famous Opera singer who just sang a concert with my mom,"

"…the night they tried to kill me," finished Margo for her.

Chapter 34

Robert Renaud Is Framed

AFTER EVERYONE was done eating, Sam turned the TV off and walked to the front of the room.

"Since we're all here, let's talk. Things are getting complicated. What started with the idea that someone was trying to get rid of Margo has now escalated to an outbreak of deaths.

"The police never sleep." He frowned at his audience, daring them to laugh. "So in the middle of the night, they picked up the drone footage that the Bay Gazette had made for the Regatta website, and I just got informed that there's been a development." Sam looked around.

"Just before the fire, the video picked up a car approaching your house, Margo, and parking next door. Let me show you." Sam plugged his computer into the TV set on the wall and punched some keys. Pretty soon they could see on screen everything the drone had filmed. An individual in a black or dark hoodie walked up to the front door of Margo's family home and entered. Then, the drone took off and circled. It continued on toward the waterfront where it picked up the images of crowds dancing silently on the Boardwalk, and the band performing their music on the seaside stage.

For a brief few seconds, the drone headed out to sea and flew over the sailboats, illuminated by myriads of hanging lights that had been strung on their masts and their sails and that were reflected in the dark waters. Then the drone turned around and took a new path.

"On its next pass," Sam continued, "it took a slightly different trajectory and picked up the back of the car. You can see it clearly here. The driver has just opened the front door of Margo's house and entered.

Luckily for us, the lab managed to magnify the license plates and trace the owner of the vehicle."

Sam stopped talking and he paused the broadcast. He fiddled with his cell phone for a few seconds, not making eye contact with anyone. But he seemed to make a decision, because he lifted his face again and looked straight at Margo.

"I'm sorry kid," he said, "but I might as well tell you straight up. The car belongs to your cousin."

"My cousin? Robert? You can't be serious, Sam. He wouldn't burn his family's house down, and he wouldn't run around killing people. He's mean, but he's not that mean." Margo stood up and crossed her arms on her chest, protesting against the idea that her cousin could kill someone.

Sam continued. "The burning down of the house could have been an accident, I grant you that. It will take a while to put together a full report, but on first inspection, the firefighter chief said it seemed like an accident. From what you said about candles, and what he observed, it's his theory that when Jenny was stabbed, she grabbed on to whatever the candles had been placed on, and by pulling them down, the dry wood or the furnishings ignited. In such an old house, it would have been unavoidable. Could that have happened?"

"Yes, I suppose so. The candles were on plates, but the plates were on a cloth on top of a chest. We placed some candles in front of my Wall Of Saints to pray for Aunt Tilly's recovery. I told Jenny to go ahead and get started lighting them because I would be right back."

"That makes sense. But it still leaves the murders."

"Yes, but Mr. Snail said that the assailant was very strong, and Robert is a wuss. I don't think he could knock anyone down."

"Well, the police will investigate that. Sit down, Margo. He hasn't been charged yet. If he has an alibi, he'll be fine. And let's let that go for now. There's no need to torment Margo until we have our facts straight. Okay then. Does anyone have anything to report?" Sam looked at his friends, who had promised to help Margo out with her investigation.

Jack walked over to Sam and took a sheet of paper out of his wallet which he proceeded to unfold and smooth out.

"I enquired about lost and missing wills, and this is what I found out. If you can find a copy or photocopy of the will, all you have to do is file a petition to have it admitted to probate and recognized as valid. Of course, the judge might deny your request. You never know. If he's friends with your aunts, you already know that he'll say no. But with some research, we could find you an impartial judge that doesn't know them and that would be willing to look into it. You know how it is in Louisiana. Much depends on who you know."

"That sounds fine, Jack, but I didn't even find a photocopy. I found the key to the safe and went into the library and opened it, but I didn't find either a will or any copies of it. And then the house burned down."

"I might be able to help you with that," Jack answered with a big grin. "Do you remember your grandfather telling you who his attorneys were?"

"Yes, I sure do."

"I went ahead and drove to New Orleans to see them, and I told them what was going on. So the senior partner is dead and all his files were shelved in the storage room, but his son—who runs the firm now—said that his dad had the habit of keeping copies of everything, just in case. His secretary is looking for a copy of the will as we speak."

"That's wonderful, Jack. Thank you so much." Margo repressed the urge to run to him and hug him.

"Hey Sam, turn the TV back on." Sam looked at Renata—who had been pretty quiet all this time playing with her cell phone—and asked her what was going on. "Just turn it on, quick."

The scene on the news segment showed the burnt-out hull of the house on East Albatross, the house that the aunts had so pretentiously named The Hornet's Nest. The reporter was retelling—again—the story of last night's fire, and the news cut to a scene of the drone's flight, bringing into focus the car parking next door and a man with a dark hoodie approaching the front door, quickly looking both ways, and then entering the house. "Moon Bay TV has just learned that the suspect is none other than the nephew of the owners, one Robert Renaud. Take us to police headquarters, Kay," he said with enthusiasm, and the next scene was of the police dragging a recalcitrant Robert up the front steps of the Town Hall. His hands had been shackled, and he was being forcefully pushed forward, but he managed to turn around and tell the reporters hounding him for a statement. "I'm innocent. I swear I'm innocent. I've been framed. Ask anyone. I was at the Yacht Club celebrating the Regatta. Hundreds of people must have seen me."

At that moment, the door to the sports room opened with a bang, and a distraught Madeline, her voice shaking, and her mascara running down her face as it mingled with her tears, stumbled in crying. "The police have arrested Robert. What am I going to do?" Saffron jumped up and went to greet her. She sat Madeline down and directed the new waiter to bring her some brandy. Then, she leaned Madeline's head gently on her shoulder and let her cry.

Chapter 35
The Forgotten Ring

MIMI POURED both of them some more Jenssen Arcana and cupped the tulip-shaped wineglass lovingly in her hands, waiting for the cognac to warm up. Dr. Gabe Gutierrez watched the news on the television, sipping on his.

"I can't believe we didn't notice the ring on his finger," he said. "But at least I'm pretty sure that after the raccoons and the roaming dogs ate part of him, any trace we might have left behind will go unnoticed."

"But dogs wouldn't eat human bodies, would they?"

"Of course they would, Mimi. You wouldn't believe how many dogs would happily eat their masters if they were hungry. I've had diabetes patients whose toes were eaten by their beloved best friends."

"Don't say that, please. That's horrible."

"Sorry. I was just trying to put you at ease. We left no trace behind. We should be safe. The blood-soaked carpeting has been incinerated, and all evidence disinfected with oxygen bleach. In a week there will not be a detectable speck of blood left in the place."

"I don't know how to thank you, Gabe."

"I owed you, Mimi. Besides, you know that I would do anything for you. Anything."

"How's Manuel?"

"He's doing fine. I put him in the guest room upstairs. He's never slept in such luxury, I don't think."

"I hope he doesn't rat us out."

"What, after you helped him get his green card? He would never do that."

Mimi continued watching the news. The last segment, where Katherine de Messian ran up to the reporter begging to see her husband, especially tore at her heart. It was devastating to lose a loved one. She knew Katherine had loved Buddy with a passion that transcended common sense even though she had a honey on the side. But then Katherine had always been very passionate, and one man had never been enough for her. Still, she didn't deserve for her husband to be dumped in the open like a bag of trash, and then be eaten by feral dogs, not like that.

And now she had a brand new problem. She looked sideways at Gabe and wondered to herself what on earth she was going to do about that.

Chapter 36

Sam And Margo Set A Trap

EVERYONE IN HALF MOON BAY, who was not down at the shore watching the sailboats getting ready for the race, was glued to their television sets watching news updates about the double tragedies of a local fire and a number of murders. Meantime, out in the bay, cannon booms signaled the official beginning of the Regatta to the delight of locals and tourists that were crowding the narrow strip of beach. In a couple of hours, sailors in their little boats would sail across Shark Bayou to the opposite shore, where they would pick up colorful batons to prove that they had made it there, and turn right back around. It was expected that the race would last until nightfall.

Margo watched the excitement around her with a sinking heart. None of the people she encountered on her way, running, laughing, happy to be alive, had any idea that four people—three of whom had been so dear to her—had died last night. Poor Jenny, who had never hurt a soul in her life, and was too young to die. And Mr. Snail, who had died trying to defend Jenny thinking that he was defending Margo. Or Rosa Nesta, the amiable cook, who would never see Jamaica—her homeland, again.

There was some doubt as to how she had died, but her passing was too much of a coincidence. Could she have been murdered? By the same person who killed Jenny and Mr. Snail? You bet. But what baffled her most was the passing of Katherine de Messian's husband. She had no idea how he figured in the whole thing, but couldn't help thinking that the four deaths were connected somehow. Half Moon Bay was, after all, a peaceful town that hadn't seen a murder in decades. How could there have been four unconnected deaths—within hours of each other? It was just too suspicious.

She tried to match Sam's long, angry, determined steps, but the man had such long legs. From the corner of her eyes she looked at all the weaponry he was carrying: his gun, all those bullets in his belt, his baton. She usually felt safe with him. Not because of the gun, but because of the vibes he projected. He was so tall and so self-assured that you just shouldn't feel scared. Yet today, she was. Very scared.

They crossed the street and entered the park. The day was resplendent, and the skies were clear. It was a perfect day for a family outing, and Margo's throat tightened as she remembered Jenny, and how excited they had been about the upcoming event. Children ran around, squealing with delight. Multicolored balloons full of helium sailed away with the wind, and the boys and girls who had allowed them to escape, admired them with wonder in their eyes as they floated ever farther toward the sky. Food vendors and souvenir salesmen peddled their wares loudly, to compete with each other. Lines of hungry customers waited in impatient lines for hot dogs, beignets, and cotton candy. And all the while, the incessant beat of the high school band, and the music from the carrousel at the other side of the park, filled the air.

Margo turned toward the beach when a collective roar reached her ears. From where she stood, facing the not-too-faraway bay, oblivious to the drama that was unfolding in the town, the sailboats began to take up line formation, and the crowds cheered.

Sam stopped and turned around to look at her. There was concern in his kind brown eyes, but Margo knew he was impatient for some action, and he didn't quite understand the depth of the sorrow in her heart. Without a word, she forced herself to put one foot in front of the other, and she kept on walking. They crossed Independence Plaza and headed toward the Cajun Dog stand. There, they stopped to eat because Sam figured she should be hungry, and he believed that on a full stomach, even the worst pain was made more bearable. But the young man at the hot dog stand asked Margo where her pretty friend was today, and Margo almost started crying again.

They found an empty bench in the shade of an old magnolia tree, and Sam urged her to sit down and get working on her dog. He ate his in two bites, wiped his mouth and hands, and stared at her until she forced herself to eat all of hers.

"Margo, we are nowhere closer to finding out who tried to kill you. It will take weeks for an investigation like this to unfold. But I'm afraid that by then our perp will have escaped. You know we don't have the resources to follow up on this for very long."

"So what are you suggesting?"

"I'm conflicted. On the one hand, I'm dying to catch whoever is behind these murders, but on the other, I'll probably have to use you as bait, and I hate to put you in danger."

"Sam, you know I'm not afraid. We have to put an end to this. They will keep coming after me unless we catch them."

"Yes, but here's the thing: the guys who were pursuing you are dead, so either there were more than those two after you, or two different people are trying to kill you."

"Isn't that a bit far out? I'm just a college kid. Why would anyone want to hurt me, to begin with?"

"I figure it's because of the money. You have too much of it."

"No, Sam. I know what you're thinking, but it doesn't add up. Yes, maybe Robert paid those two guys to get rid of me so he could inherit grandpa's money. I can see Robert outsourcing my disappearance because he is too much of a coward to do the killing himself."

"You're young, Margo, and you haven't seen what I have seen. You wouldn't believe what human beings are capable of when pressured into a corner."

"But with his bare hands or with a knife? No, he would have never had the guts to do that."

"I don't know, I don't know," Sam said, and he ruffled his hair up in frustration. "Maybe it's something else altogether. Maybe you know something you shouldn't. Maybe you saw something you shouldn't have. I have no idea. Let's see what we have. You come to town, and Madeline says she overhears someone mention that a Kathy Mason put a hit on you."

"Yes. And we never did find out who she was."

"Then, you and Jenny are almost run over by the guy in the jeep."

"Right."

"Maybe they were just trying to scare you. They chased you at the Opera House, and then they chased you from the market, but you never actually got hurt."

"That's true. And then, they got killed. So what are you saying?"

"That maybe the people who tried to scare you were different than the people who killed your friend and burned down your aunts' house. I've been thinking. There's a way to smoke the guilty person out, whoever he or she is."

"And how do you propose that we do that?"

"Well, I had an idea. You'll probably hate it. We're going to let the press interview you."

That afternoon, the Sunday of the Regatta, Margo stood on the steps leading up to the Opera House wearing one of Saffron's more conservative pantsuits and took questions from the media. The reporters were unusually respectful. They knew that Margo's mother had been a celebrity, and that, even without going into too many details, she was one of the richest people among them. Reporters—knowing the importance of respecting those that signed their paychecks—obediently asked the questions that Sam had proposed for them.

"If you know who murdered the people in your house, why don't you tell us now?"

"Because tomorrow morning I'm going to the police station to sign a statement, and until then it would be irresponsible to mention names."

"Fair enough."

"But meet me here tomorrow morning at ten, and I'll tell you what I know, and how I discovered the identity of the murderer."

"And will you be able to prove it?"

"Absolutely. The murderer made one mistake, and he left something behind that will prove without the shadow of a doubt that he did it."

"Will you be turning that in to the police?"

"Of course. Tomorrow morning. It's regatta Sunday. I believe the police should be allowed to have the day off like everyone else. In the meantime, it's safe in my purse." Margo gave the cameras a dazzling smile and patted her purse.

"Are you going to be attending the festivities?"

"I am going to watch the race, but from the Lookout. There's a stone bench up there that gives a perfect view of the bay. My heart is heavy with sadness, and I'm not in the mood to be surrounded by crowds right now."

Margo stepped down from the stairs and walked toward the beach while the cameras followed her for a while. They would broadcast the interview every half hour that afternoon calling it *breaking news—this just in.* It was a simple plan, but unless the murderer was brilliant, they might be able to pull it off. Meantime, her purse had enough food and water to sustain her through the afternoon. And she would take turns reading and watching sailboats. Hopefully, it didn't take too long.

Chapter 37

Tony Toups

MARGO SAT ON THE STONE BENCH at the Lookout holding the tooled red leather tome of Shakespeare's Sonnets with care. It was a beautiful old book. She passed her fingertips on the deep etchings filled in gold that spelled out his name and pondered whether she should even bother opening it. She knew well enough that she wouldn't understand any of it, but a sense of guilt always drove her to pick up a Classic just because it had such an important place in history. But bah, humbug.

The day had continued being glorious. It obviously didn't care about her personal sorrow and gave the world that perfect blue sky in which not a blemish, not a cloud would dare fly by. A flotilla of Laughing Gulls flew overhead, showing off their white bodies, red beaks, and their raucous kee-agh call, which sounds so much like a high-pitched ha ha ha, flapping their wings, heading east. After all this was over, she too would fly away. East sounded good. Anywhere but here sounded good.

She watched the sailboats for a while as they got smaller and smaller and finally disappeared into the horizon, and bit into her second candy bar. Then she made an effort at the Sonnets and read out loud,

Suche vayn thought as wonted to myslede me:

In desert hope by well assured mone:

Maketh me from compayne to live alone:

In folowing hir whome reason bid me fle.

But she gave up. The words made no sense, and the book was too heavy, and the warm afternoon sun made her sleepy. Sounds from the cheering crowd by the beachfront echoed up to where she sat. Dogs barking, kids squealing with delight, it all made for the illusion of comfort, safety, and happiness. She sort of closed her eyes and thought about Jenny and better times, of years of friendship and all the good and bad memories. Then she remembered their botched plans for the future and was just about to doze off when a rustling in the bushes woke her up.

She turned her body toward the noise and saw a very young, very blonde man appearing from behind the shrubbery and walking with determined steps toward her. He was very tall and powerfully built, and Margo immediately thought bodybuilder. But he didn't look threatening, just rather shy instead, and Margo wondered if this was the person she had been expecting.

The young man sat down uninvited next to her on the bench and started to talk to her as if they had known each other forever.

"This view is breathtaking," he said. "It's always been my favorite spot. I used to come here after school—way before this bench and the guardrail were ever built—to eat my snack. Back then, I thought I would be a sailor one day and travel to the far ends of the world."

"What happened?"

"Oh, life happened." The young man shrugged despondently. "My dad died, and I had to go work to help my mom out, you know, help feed the younger kids."

"I'm sorry," Margo said. "Somehow life never turns out to be the way we expected. My name is Margo."

"I know. I'm Tony." The young man faced the water and sighed. The sailboats were quickly vanishing into the afternoon haze. "I'm sorry," he said sadly. His knees were slightly apart as he sat, and he had clasped his hands together as if in prayer.

"Sorry about what, Tony?"

"It was an accident."

"What was an accident?"

The young man's breath had quickened. Margo wondered if she should feel afraid of sitting next to such a sad, friendly guy who nevertheless exuded an air of vague danger. If this was the man who had gone on that murderous rampage, she could easily be next. Yet all Margo could see was a troubled, shy, gentle giant, a feeling that seemed to override her better judgment. "What was an accident, Tony?" she asked again.

"The fire, everything. I just needed the letter back. Kathy wanted her letter back, and I promised her I would get it."

"What letter?"

"The letter. The letter. She didn't want to give it back."

"What letter?"

The young man rummaged in his pocket and handed her a crumpled letter with a hand as big as a dinner plate. Blond hairs on the back of his hand shone in the setting sun, and Margo shivered with fear thinking about what those hands were capable of, but she accepted the sheet of paper. She opened it and smoothed it down on her lap. There was nothing on it but a couple of sentences. It was written to Beth. Obviously, Aunt Beth. Her hands shook as she read it out loud. 'Dear Beth, thanks for letting me know. Tony will take care of everything.'

"That's it? This was the reason all those people had to die? The cook, Mr. Snail, and my friend Jenny? For a miserable two sentences?" Margo sensed that she shouldn't have raised her voice so abruptly. Her anger had an effect on Tony. All of a sudden, the shyness and the friendliness were gone. His eyes went dead cold, and his nostrils quivered as if he was sniffing his prey. Folding the page again, Margo got up and slowly—very carefully—walked away from the bench. But Tony got up too, with a quicker move than you would have expected from such a big man.

"That's not how it happened," he said angrily and took a step toward her. Make him talk, Sam had said, but Margo was getting very scared. Still, she had to make him confess.

"How did it happen, then?"

"I went to see the cook. She was trying to blackmail Kathy. Why did she have to do that? I asked for the letter nicely, but then I had to force her because she didn't want to give it. Then she threatened to call the police, and I couldn't let her. I had to stop her."

"And then what, you just went upstairs and murdered those other people who had never laid eyes on you? You were safe then. Why didn't you just leave? I don't understand?" Margo took another step back and Tony matched hers, except his step was so much longer, and now he was getting closer and closer to her.

"No. No," he shouted. "You don't understand. Kathy wanted you dead. I had promised. She was going to buy the gym for me if I did what she said. She swore she would buy me the gym. Can you imagine, me with my own gym? My mom is old, and she still needs help. With my own gym we could have a good life. As good a life as Kathy has."

"So what happened then?" Margo asked.

"I went upstairs, looking for you. But that man tried to stop me, so I had to kill him. I found you in the attic. I thought I killed you, but I had never seen you before except in pictures and I thought it was you, but it wasn't, and now you're not dead at all, and Kathy is very angry at me."

"Stop, Tony. Don't get any closer, or I'll fall over the cliff."

"That's not a cliff, silly. It's only like ten feet."

"It is a cliff. There are those horrible pointy rocks down there, and if you keep coming any closer, I'm going to fall on them and kill myself."

"Not a bad idea. Kathy wants you dead. If I push you over, they will think it was an accident, and Kathy will love me again and forgive me, and buy me the gym."

"Oh, come on Tony. You don't really want to kill me," she said, now dangerously close to the guardrail, trying to negotiate, to reason with the young man. Where on earth was Sam? Didn't he have enough on him already to step out of the bushes and arrest this guy before he pushed her over?"

"Give me your bag, Margo."

"What bag?"

"The evidence. The proof that I killed those people. You told the reporter that the proof was in your bag."

"I was bluffing. I don't have any proof."

"Give me the bag." Tony was so close now that Margo could feel his hot, sour breath on her face. He stuck his enormous hand out and grabbed her purse by the straps. With his other hand, he slowly began pushing her against the guardrail.

THE BURNING FIRE OF GREED

She walked backward until her waist touched the metal rail and she stopped. This is it, she told herself. All the plans for the future, her love for Jack, her sorrow for Jenny, and the loneliness that had followed her since childhood, this was where it ended. There was no Sam, no rescue squad, just little Margo and this shy, crazy lunatic, and the sky and the sea, and the Laughing Gulls mocking her for having failed. She closed her eyes and said a quick prayer to Saint Jude, the patron saint of lost causes, and was about ready for the void, and for eternity when she heard Sam's voice yelling stop, stop.

Suddenly, Tony stopped pushing and turned around. Good old Sam had come to her rescue after all.

"It's over, Tony. Let her go."

"Gee, Sam, you took your sweet time."

"Sorry, Margo. The boss wanted to talk to me. He didn't let me go until I explained to him what we were trying to do." Then he turned to Tony. "Come on, big guy, turn around. You're under arrest."

"I'm not going to jail, Sam. No way. I'll die in there. I can't stand to be locked up." He shook his handsome blond head and kept walking backward. He was now just a couple of inches from the edge of the cliff. And there was so much despair in his voice that despite what he had done, Margo's heart went out to him. "I'm sorry for hurting your friend, Margo. I'm not a bad person. I had never hurt anyone in my life before." Despair and hopelessness filled his eyes, and he turned around to look down toward the rocks as if picking the sharpest one to fall on.

Meantime they hadn't noticed that someone was running toward them screaming, waving her arms above her head. "Stop, Tony, please don't jump."

As if frozen in a medieval tableau, all three stopped moving and stared at the newcomer. She was tall and blonde, middle-aged. Margo could tell because she didn't have the quick fluid movements of younger people. She hobbled more than ran. As she got closer, Margo remembered the recital. She remembered thinking that Katherine de Messian reminded her of Wagner's Viking women, and the pieces fell in place. Katherine de Messian, wife of Buddy Mason. Kathy Mason. Kathy

Mason who had put a hit on her. Katherine the Messian, who wanted her dead.

"Tony, don't jump," she pleaded with the young man, ignoring both Sam and Margo. "Come, honey, step away from the edge. Take my hand."

"But I let you down. You won't love me anymore. You said so."

"I didn't mean it, Tony. Of course, I'll love you. I'll always love you. Come on. Give me your hand."

Tony looked at Katherine sadly and then at Margo. "I'm really sorry I killed your friend. I hope you'll forgive me one day." Then he turned toward the sea, and in one quick graceful move, jumped over the guardrail and opened his arms as if he was going to fly away. And for a brief few seconds, he did. He cleared the rail and he remained suspended for a heartbeat in the horizon, his face lifted to the sky, his eyes closed. Then his heavy body fell flat, and they heard a thump and a horrible crunch as his body was pierced by the jagged rocks below. It hadn't been a high jump, but everyone knew it was a deadly one. At least he would never be locked away in jail. He died free.

Margo tried to get a grip on her conflicting emotions, but all she could do was shiver uncontrollably from the shock. There had been so many deaths. So many pointless deaths. And she was homeless and back at square one, and she wished dearly that she had never come to spend the summer in Half Moon Bay.

Poor Katherine wailed as if she was performing the death scene of the slave-girl Liù in Turandot. She didn't even fight when Sam led her away. She was devastated. Within a few minutes, Margo heard police sirens and the ambulance and realized she had been left behind, sitting alone on the bench..

Chapter 38

Katherine's Heartbreak

"WHY KATHERINE? WHY?" It was Saffron, yelling at Katherine—the now-infamous Opera singer. Saffron held Margo's hand protectively as if she was her little sister. "What could have been so grave that you had to have her killed?"

"You wouldn't understand. I spent years having to listen to Buddy wail about his kid. Margo this, Margo that. I was sick and tired of it."

"What do you mean?"

"Buddy was Margo's dad, didn't you know? That harlot Nicole, as soon as she was old enough to have a boyfriend, she wouldn't stop flirting with him, teasing him. And Buddy couldn't resist her. She was graceful, beautiful, younger. Everything I was not. And he got Nicole pregnant. He was going to leave me for her. He was madly in love with her, but she said no, she didn't want to get married. She had great plans for the future, and they didn't include Buddy, and so she skipped town. After a few years, we heard Nicole had had a baby and was on her way to becoming famous.

"Then he changed his will." Margo stared in horror at Katherine, sitting in the single cell of the tiny police department with her makeup running, and her hair in tatters, looking like an aging scarecrow. Time had not been kind to the famous singer. She looked years older than she should have, and continuous tours and performances had drained the life out of her. Now, her husband's death followed within hours by her lover's death had devastated her. She looked like an old woman.

She had refused to talk to the police saying she would wait for her lawyer, but when she saw Saffron and Margo, she broke down. Hers had been a lonely life at the top. Friends, Margo's mom used to tell her, they come flocking to you because you have money and power, and not because they love you. And so it was with Katherine.

"I couldn't take it any longer. I waited too long to have children, and then it was too late. So Buddy became obsessed with getting Margo into his life. He still loved Nicole even though she was dead. Can you believe that? For years she had been the ideal woman, mother of his only child, the one that got away. I couldn't compete with that. And that stupid will. He loved the dead woman's child more than he loved his own wife. I was brokenhearted and didn't have anyone to turn to for comfort. Then one day, I met Tony. Sweet Tony. He was kind and compliant, and he loved me. Always willing to do anything I asked. Then I had the idea. Get rid of the kid once and for all. Tony would do it, I was sure."

"But you have so much money, Katherine, why did the will bother you so much?"

"It was not the money, Saffron. It really wasn't. I had hated Nicole since the day she came into our lives and ruined our marriage, and when I heard that her child was back in town, I couldn't take it any longer. But I never thought I would lose both of them. And now it's all over for me." Saffron nodded but didn't say anything.

Chapter 39
Farewell To Jenny

WHEN THEY STEPPED out into the sun, Margo covered her eyes with an arm and squinted. She would have to get some sunglasses. The sky was always too bright in Half Moon Bay.

Walking fast, trying to keep up with Saffron's longer steps, she headed for St. Quintian's Church. Storms and hurricanes had been kind to the old church. It stood in more or less all its former glory, defying the decay and the wrath of the ages. It had turned out to be every bit as resilient as the mysterious 5th-century saint it had been named after.

Margo climbed the marble steps with a heavy heart. She looked up at the familiar words carved deeply into the stone lintel above the columns, those pillars that seemed to elevate her humble prayer to heaven: *Omnipotens Sempiterne Deus, Miserere Famulis Tuis.* Margo read the Latin invocation softly to herself as she always did, trying to absorb the true meaning of the mysterious words as if they really held the secret to salvation. And she wondered if the Almighty and everlasting God would have mercy on Jenny's soul even though she never received the last rites nor did she ever have a chance to confess her sins.

She quickly dipped her fingers in the holy water font by the door and made the sign of the cross, mumbling a *Bless Me, Father*. Saffron was way ahead of her, already about to sit in the front pew, and Margo shuffled along the nave, carefully avoiding the bier that held Jenny's white and gold casket. Renata was there with her mother Mimi on the other side, and so was Madeline, sitting with two of her three children, who against all odds appeared to be well behaved for the occasion.

Margo sat down by Saffron and made an effort to collect her thoughts, leaving all mundane worries behind. She inhaled the scent of incense that always permeated the church. Even though she sometimes questioned religion and was not as assiduous in showing up on Sundays for Mass as she should, she loved the peace she felt sitting in the ancient wooden pews, surrounded by beautiful colonial statues of saints and the gilded, carved intricacies that ornamented the pretty church.

The organist and the choir were warming up, up there in the choir loft, filling the air with ancient hymns and Gregorian Chant. Father Armand despised modern Church Music and always managed to persuade the choir director to perform more traditional—if old fashioned—liturgical pieces. And for that she was grateful. She closed her eyes, and her soul was carried away by the *Miserere*.

Finally—after a lot of shuffling—everyone settled down, and the Mass began. Margo exhaled with relief. Until the last minute, she wasn't sure that Father Armand would be willing to go through with it. He glared at her with antipathy as he recited the *Requiem æternam dona eis, Domine; et lux perpetua luceat eis*. She had made an enemy in her place of worship, but there was no turning back. Father Armand was a stubborn man who insisted on following the Rites of the Catholic Church to the letter, and Jenny wasn't Catholic. But she was every bit as stubborn as the priest was. It had been a tour-de-force squabble accompanied by threats. And ugly words were said, mostly by her, much to her embarrassment. Knowing certain secrets about his past—thanks to Saffron's gossip grapevine—helped, so here they all were, saying goodbye to her dear friend.

The bier holding Jenny's body was almost close enough to touch. For a second she felt that Jenny was calling out to her, and she repressed the urge to run to her and open the coffin, to make sure that she was truly dead, that she wasn't being buried alive. With an aching heart, she focused on staying sane and paid attention to Father Armand's words.

The sun shone through the plain glass window above Christ on the Cross, behind the altar, and touched the white coffin gently as it lay in the middle of the transept, covered by pale white lilies, giving it an otherworldly brilliance. It should have all been so peaceful and comforting, but her heart wasn't in it. She was having a hard time letting go of the anger. Her heart was broken. Over and over she remembered Jenny, burned and bleeding, lying dead in her arms. She kept pushing the memory away, but sweet, innocent Jenny had died in her place. And for that, she couldn't forgive herself.

She looked around. The church was almost empty. Not many people had really known about Jenny. Rosa Nesta and Snail had seemed to be fond of her, and they would have been here, but they too were dead. Jenny's young aunt and her cousins had been invited, and should have made an effort, but were nowhere to be seen. So, in the end, it was just them: her handful of new friends and a few stragglers that had wandered into the church out of curiosity. Poor Jenny, unloved in life, ignored in death. But hey, now she was going to be buried in her own Fontaine family mausoleum, close to her mom. And at least in death, Jenny should feel loved and would never be lonely again.

Listening to Father Armand talk about love, loss, and belonging, made her think about her own life. Her mind wandered as his monotone voice droned on and on. Maybe it was time to give up this constant desire to run away and instead find a place to live and settle down. She felt more at home in Half Moon Bay than she did anywhere else. She had friends now, and she had two cats to care for, and after all, her loved ones were buried here, and she hated to leave them behind.

Jenny's pretty white casket was carried solemnly out of the church by Sam and Jack, and a couple of members of the church she had never seen before. All in all, it was a pretty day for a funeral: cheerful, sunny, with plenty of birds singing, and a cloud of butterflies fluttering among the plentiful flowers in the graveyard. It was as a good a day to be buried as any. She hung on to Saffron's arm and strolled over to the mausoleum. Madeline—walking on her other side—was crying softly, drying up her tears with a small frilly handkerchief. Her two children out of three, perhaps sensing the overwhelming importance of the moment, followed obediently in silence. Madeline was carrying a big cross herself, on those slender, narrow shoulders. Her future looked as bleak and uncertain as her own.

Margo sighed. It was going to be a long and sad week. She had purchased plots for Rosa Nesta and for Snail—who had no family either that she knew of—close to the back of the cemetery, where they would lay quietly under the shade of centenarian oaks for all eternity, close together, side by side, so they could keep each company in death as they had done in life. And after that, she would see. The future was a *tabula rasa*, thankfully an empty slate, and it was up to her to find something worthy to fill it with.

After the funeral, she and Sam had lunch together, and then—armed with a bucket load of legal papers—went to visit Robert in the big house. She braced herself. It wasn't going to be pretty.

Chapter 40
Robert Moves

A MAID OPENED THE DOOR, and she entered. The house was as quiet as the mausoleum she had just left. This was the house her mom had grown up in. Up there on the second floor somewhere was the room in which she had slept and read and studied.

It was an old house, run-down, still showing the damage of that famous storm that had rumbled through town and decimated most of it. The lace on the curtains that covered the windows appeared moth-eaten and stained by mildew. The windows themselves were made with ancient heavy leaded glass that barely let any sunshine through.

She took a few steps forward. Immediately she was startled by the way the floorboards creaked. Then, she noticed that the wallpaper was rotting off the walls, peeling down in tight little curls, leaving empty spots that looked infested with a greenish, spreading virus. The oriental rugs were threadbare, the paintings and mirrors around her, stained with age. She was appalled at the state of neglect everywhere. Not that it didn't have that feel of a rarely-visited museum, including the dusty smell of decay, but for crying out loud, did Robert have to let the place fall apart like this? It was going to take forever to get it restored.

"You never had it renovated," she told her cousin—surprised— when she saw him walk out of the darkened back of the house toward her.

"I was going to. But I kind of like it like this, you know? Old, full of history. What would restorers do? They would come in and gut the place. Throw everything out. Renew it, but kill its past. There are so many memories in this house. I grew up here, you know. Your mom was always singing, and the grownups were always telling her to tone it down." Robert laughed. "She was too loud and cheerful for their taste. But I loved to hear her sing. I learned the piano so I could play for her, to accompany her. She had the most exquisite voice: high, perfectly clear, like drops of diamonds clinking in a crystal glass.

"But this was not a happy home. She got tired of the nagging and the bickering, and she left as soon as she was old enough. My brother left too. They left me behind with those bitter, angry people. I despised them for that." Robert walked into the living room, and she followed him. She looked sadly at the strips of lace curtains that hung in tatters. In a way, it was a merciful thing, this penumbra, this semi-darkness that managed to add a small amount of romantic glamour to an otherwise threadbare, neglected room.

"I love this house, and I hate it," Robert said, sweeping an arm to encompass everything around him. "The memories are all either too good or too bad. How many times have I told myself that I have to get out of here, to break the hold that it has on me? But I can't seem to. My life is woven into its history. Or it is the other way around? I don't know. But I don't think I can leave, even though I know that you're here to tell me that I must. I've been unmasked, and now I have to pay the price."

"Why don't you take my offer and buy a house near me? We'll convert the inheritance into a Family Trust. You could run it. God knows there's plenty of money for all of us. And we could try to be a family. Every Tuesday afternoon and every Sunday after church y'all could come to the house, and after dinner, play the piano, and I'll sing for you. Just like we used to."

"But you would still want me to leave this house."

"Yes, because you have no interest in having it restored. You want to live in the past. And Madeline and the kids deserve better."

"Why don't you just say what you're not saying, which is that you want the house because it's yours?"

Margo nodded. She did want the house. It was the house where her mother had lived. The house that her ancestor Francesc Fontayn—the pirate—had built. Yes, Robert was right. This was her house, and she wanted it.

"There's no need to answer, Margo. I can see it in your eyes. But I can't take your offer. I feel resentful because you discovered that we stole your inheritance, and still you don't hate me." Robert clasped his hands behind his back and walked to the window. Outside, the sea was sparkling under the shining sun. But the cheerfulness refused to come indoors. "This is new territory for me," he added, sounding baffled. "Someone who actually doesn't hate me."

"Please accept," she begged, following him to the window. "Madeline is a sweet person. She doesn't deserve to live in poverty—God knows where—when there's so much family money available. Besides, what about the aunts?"

"If I have to go, I'm going alone. Madeline won't be coming with me. She's told me that she still loves me, but she wants to stay in Half Moon Bay, so if you can help her, I'll be grateful. But the aunts, well, they decided they've had enough of family life, and they're moving to a nursing home."

"And what will you do?"

"I think I'm going to try to find my brother. He's out there somewhere if he isn't dead. I need to get away from here, and from the monster I've become. I hope you'll forgive me one day."

"Robert, please don't go away."

"Look around. This place is my life. If I can't live here, I have to go somewhere else, far away. I can't compromise. Anyway, I have very little worth packing. Give me another couple of days, and I'll be out of here. And by the way, the will's in the safe."

"In the library, behind the painting of the seascape, in between the two big windows that look out at the bay."

Robert turned around suddenly and looked back at Margo with a perplexed expression, his eyebrows raised in surprise. "And how would you know that?" he asked.

"Lila told me. Remember her?"

"Oh yes, I do remember her. I had no idea she was still alive."

Chapter 41

Jack

IT WAS THE PERFECT BEACH DAY. She closed her eyes and faced the sun, and listened to the world around her. People were chatting everywhere. Nobody stayed indoors on days like these unless they really had to. She smiled. She could hear that someone was opening a can of soda, someone crushing a paper wrapper. With her eyes still closed, she played at identifying the sounds. Children running, their voices coming and going as if they were running back and forth along the beach.

Dogs, barking at the surf. Those must be the two German Shepherds that she saw arrive with the elderly gentleman. *Mojitos, mojitos,* a vendor yelled as he passed her by, throwing sand on her towel. After passing by her a couple more times, the vendor gave up and moved on.

She continued listening to the surf with her eyes closed, filtering out all the other sounds around her. She remembered a funny story Rosa Nesta had told her.

"Rosa, you have a gold tooth," she had asked.

"Oh yes, from the time my cousin Roque knocked it out when I told him no."

"No to what, Mrs. Cook?" Jenny had asked innocently.

"Never you mind that, Miss Jenny" she had answered. "Just eat your rice."

"And so you got a gold tooth?"

"Yes. My mother, rest her soul, didn't want the neighbors to think that we were poor—which we were—so she got me the gold tooth. So that the neighbors would think that we could afford such an extravagance. We barely ate for a whole month while she paid the dentist off."

Margo laughed quietly. The rhythmic pounding of the waves on the shore hypnotized her, and the sounds around her faded away and she fell asleep.

Until that is, a big blob of drool fell on her face and woke her up. She sat up startled and looked straight into the face of Jack's big dog. "Paco," she gurgled happily, "what are you doing here?"

Jack and Paco plopped themselves on the sand next to her, and Jack put his arms around her.

"I came to say goodbye." Margo's heart skipped a beat.

"What do you mean goodbye? I just found you again, and now you're leaving?" Jack hung his head sadly.

"I'm sorry, Fontaine, but I did something really stupid a while back, and now I can't change it. I have to go."

"What did you do, Jack?"

"I lost a bet, and I joined the army."

"Seriously?"

"Yes. It seemed like a good idea at the time. I was overcome by patriotic fervor when my cousin got himself blown up in Iraq, and I wanted vengeance really badly. I bet my drinking buddies that I was going to go over there and kill whoever had done this to my cousin, so out of bravado, we went to the recruiting office, and I signed up. But then I sobered up and realized that I myself might die—which I don't want to do—so I went back and tried to change things, but they said it was too late. I had signed, and now I had to go."

"No, you can't do that. It's not fair."

"No, it's not fair. I don't even think I'm cut out for military life. But I have no choice. But listen, don't be sad. I have a proposal for you." Jack grabbed his jacket and stuck his hand in one of the pockets. He took out a small black velvet box, and Margo's heart started jumping around in her chest like it had gone wild.

"Now don't get too excited," Jack said quickly when he saw her reaction. "This was my grandmother's ring. I slipped it out of the safe without permission, so don't go showing everyone."

"Without permission, Jack? So it's not yours to give?"

"Well, yes it is mine, I guess. I'm the only one left in the family, pretty much, but my uncle's out of town, and I had to hurry up and talk to you before I left. So here's the deal."

"The deal?"

"Yes. Quit interrupting me, Fontaine. I have to leave, and there's no guarantee that I'll make it back, but take this ring as an engagement ring, and when I come back, if I come back alive and not feet first, let's get married."

"Wow, this is the most romantic proposal I've ever heard," Margo said facetiously. But Jack misunderstood, and he laughed.

"I knew you'd love the idea. Now we're like those couples from the fifties war movies, and we'll get married on a whim and live happily ever after." He grabbed Margo and gave her the most passionate kiss she could have dreamed of. Her eyes were still tightly shut, and she was already dreaming of a creamy white wedding dress and an enormous bouquet of flowers in her arms when suddenly Jack let go. Then, he and Paco hopped up. Jack wiped the sand off his trousers and smiled at her. "And now, I really must go. See you around, Fontaine."

"See you around?" she repeated, trying to figure what had just happened. But by the time she reacted and got up to follow, they were long gone. All she could see was the tip of Paco's tail wagging enthusiastically before they turned a corner. And then, as if she had been dreaming, they were gone.

Chapter 42

A New Beginning

MARGO WALKED up the stairs to the big house on the beach, carrying the cats—each in one basket—one in each hand. It was a momentous occasion, and somewhere in her imagination, a marching band played a Sousa march for her.

The house was now empty. Rundown and empty, but in her eyes, it was already shining with all the glory a restoration would give her. It would be as elegant and magnificent as it had once been.

She put the baskets down and touched the door: the carved wood, the tooled copper doorknob, the intricately cut leaded window, and finally the keyhole. This was it. It was not what she had initially set out to do, but it was a good ending. She would stay in Half Moon Bay, originally settled by her ancestors. She would restore their pride and joy. She would keep the weeds off their tombs in the cemetery and bring them flowers for special occasions, and she would commission a stained glass window for the church in the family's name. Yes. She would make her mother proud.

The little cats mewled in their baskets. They were getting impatient. *Don't worry*, she told them. *I'll love you every bit as much as your mom did, and I'll take good care of you.* She took the key out of her pocket and she looked around. No need to be bashful, she told herself. This is your house now. And with a deep breath for courage, she opened the door and stepped inside. She was home.

Don't miss the next Margo Fontaine Mystery:

The Vanishing Bloodstain

Chapter 10

Carolyn's Ghosts

CAROLYN SIGHED WITH RELIEF when the last of her guests closed the door behind them. It was becoming harder and harder to lead a double life: sweet and loving grandmother, neighbor, and friend by day, terrified owner of haunted plantation home by night.

Her guests had stayed too long, and she was exhausted. She needed to lie down to stretch her stiff, aching body. Her head was throbbing again tonight. The sharp pain behind her eyes banged in her veins to the rhythm of her steps as she walked toward the staircase.

Sharmila turned the lights off downstairs one by one as she retreated to the servants' quarters in the back of the house, and Carolyn was left all alone in the heavy darkness. She blinked repeatedly, adjusting her eyes to the dark. How she wished that she hadn't sent everyone home, but she couldn't bear their cloying company any longer.

She slowly climbed the endless staircase that led to her second-story bedroom, counting the creaking stairs as she went. Every year it got harder and harder for her old knees to do so much climbing, and she knew she had to face the possibility of moving to one of the bedrooms downstairs. But she was terrified of the downstairs at night. Because—in spite of what everyone thought—there was something down there that came out at night; something that she didn't understand, that slithered about in a foggy miasma during the dark hours of the night, rustling like roaches trapped in a wall.

Carolyn didn't dare sleep downstairs. She knew those ghosts were there for her. They always had been. They had pursued her from country to country across the globe without respite. Some nights, she wished that God would take her already and put her out of her misery. But she was also afraid of dying.

She reached the last rung and refused to look behind her. Once or twice—many years ago—she had dared and had watched, terrified, the fog rising behind her, and saw the things squirming in it, unspeakable things that made no sense. No, Carolyn didn't look behind her.

She entered her bedroom as fast as she could and locked the door with the old bolt and the new one that Pierre had installed for her recently. She listened with her ear to the door. Her breath was coming in jagged gasps and her hands were shaking. She had a feeling that they were down there, waiting for her, looking upward toward her bedroom door, hoping that she would open it and come out. She wondered—like she did every night—what they would do to her if they ever caught her. As she got older and slower, she also wondered why they never had. Maybe they enjoyed the fear they brought out in her. Maybe they laughed at her as she scrambled with difficulty up the steep rungs of the staircase, and that was all they wanted from her.

She was so tired tonight. Maybe she would be able to fall asleep. She changed into her nightgown and climbed in bed with her Bible as she did every single night. Sometimes, the fear was so unbearable that she didn't close her eyes at all until the first rays of the sun came out. Other times, she was too tired to be afraid. Then she fell asleep with the lights on, with the Bible open on her chest. She dearly hoped this would be one of those nights. She started reading fervently.

Then she heard the noises. They had arrived. They were down there. She could hear them whispering, and they were dragging something on the floor. Then, she heard what she had never heard before: the stairs creaking one by one. They had never come upstairs, these ghosts, never in her whole life. But they were tonight. She could hear them. One step, another step, and then another, and her heart was pounding so hard that it was about to jump out of her chest. Please let me die, God, please let me die, she prayed, but God didn't need any more dead bodies tonight, and the footsteps kept coming closer and closer.

Carolyn huddled under her quilt, afraid to breathe, afraid to move, and prayed like she never had before. She heard the creaking floorboards in front of her bedroom door, and someone trying the knob. With eyes that couldn't tear themselves away, she stared at the doorknob as it turned from side to side. She felt that she was about to lose all self-control and begin screaming like she had never screamed before.

Thanks for reading! Please add a short review on Amazon and let me know what you thought!

About the Author

Agnes Makóczy is a freelance writer and adventure traveler. She's the author of the Margo Fontaine Mysteries, a series that takes place in the fictional seaside town of Half Moon Bay, in South Louisiana.

Ms. Makóczy loves to write. She carries her computer everywhere and finds inspiration for her stories in the places she travels to. After brief attempts at Romance Novels and one Health book, she's had to face the truth: she loves Murder Mysteries the best.

To read about her other books and upcoming works, please visit:

www.agnes-makoczy.com

www.ingramcontent.com/pod-product-compliance
Lightning Source LLC
Chambersburg PA
CBHW050931120626
46552CB00001B/154